hectic
ethics

hectic
ethics

stories by **francisco hinojosa**

Translated from the Spanish by Kurt Hollander

city lights books
san francisco

HECTIC ETHICS
English translations ©1998 by Kurt Hollander

First City Lights Edition, 1998
All Rights Reserved

Cover design and photography by Rex Ray
Book design by Elaine Katzenberger
Typography by Harvest Graphics

These stories first appeared in Spanish in the following Mexican
editions: *Informe negro*, Fondo de Cultura Económica ©1987, 1995;
Memorias segadas de un hombre en el fondo bueno, Ediciones Heliópolis
©1995; *Cuentos héticos*, Editorial Joaquín Mortiz, ©1996

This edition was made possible by a
grant from the U.S./Mexico Fund for
Culture and the institutions which
support it—The Rockefeller Foundation,
Fundación Cultural Bancomer, and Fondo
Nacional para la Cultura y las Artes.

Library of Congress Cataloging-in-Publication Data

Hinojosa, Francisco.
    Hectic ethics / by Francisco Hinojosa ; translated from the
Spanish by Kurt Hollander.
        p.   cm.
    ISBN 0-87286-347-6
    1. Hinojosa, Francisco—Translations into English.
    I. Hollander, Kurt. II. Title.
PQ7298.18.I65H44   1998
863—dc21   98-35165
                                                        CIP

City Lights Books are available to bookstores through our primary
distributor: Subterranean Company, P. O. Box 160, 265 S. 5th St., Monroe,
OR 97456. Tel: (541)-847-5274. Toll-free orders (800)-274-7826. Fax:
(541)-847-6018. Our books are also available through library jobbers and
regional distributors. For personal orders and catalogs, please write to
City Lights Books, 261 Columbus Avenue, San Francisco, CA 94133, or
visit us on the World Wide Web at: www.citylights.com.

CITY LIGHTS BOOKS are edited by Lawrence Ferlinghetti and Nancy
J. Peters and published at the City Lights Bookstore, 261 Columbus
Avenue, San Francisco, CA 94133.

contents

an example of beauty

I STROVE TO CREATE SOMETHING BEAUTIFUL. I WANTED this Beautiful thing to be Beautiful in and of itself, regardless of the ideology of the observer. Regardless even of their opinions or their aesthetic tendencies, regardless whether they were Eastern or Western, an old-timer from the country or a student from the city. I rejected Abstract Art from the start, as it had successfully managed to confound me for the last two decades of my Existence. I then attempted a portrait of a nude, but I couldn't find a body that was sufficiently Beautiful to breathe Life into my project. I tried my hand at Cubism, which I had always loathed, in the hopes that the Perfect Aesthetic could be derived from an error of my Appreciation. Nonetheless, the outcome was a little less than monstrous and a little more than unpleasant. It had a slight touch of Braque from his years of Neglect. I was then called upon to head the National School of Fine Arts, and I accepted because the truth is I had always wanted to be Director in order to impose my Criteria. I asked the instructors to promote the creation of Beautiful Works among their students. As a result I received a great deal of criticism and protest. After three months the situation became impossible; I resigned and returned to my Studio. A student of mine, a young woman, offered to pose for me, and I made four Paintings of her before I finally gave in and kissed her mouth and neck many times, as can be imagined. The class I held the following day in the School (I had resigned as Director, not as instructor) was based on the idea of having a physical, even carnal, contact with the model being painted in order to allow Beauty to emanate from the work. My other students, a bunch of idiots, misunderstood my words and went to the new director to complain about my politically incorrect behavior. He reprimanded me and I criticized him and lobbied against him, but in the end I was fired from the School and I returned once again to my Studio, to my Idea of Beauty and to Vodka on the rocks. Although my young student continued to visit me and let me kiss her with Simplicity some times, with Passion other times, I no longer Painted her because I was now Studying a truly Beautiful Papaya that I had bought in the market. Even if the idea of a Still Life didn't conform to my Idea of Art, I accepted the fact that the Intuition that led me toward this fruit could only be described as Artistic, or to put it another way, as authentically Spontaneous. After seven weeks, I finally finished the Canvas. It was (and still is today) a Rotten Papaya that truly radiated (that radiates) that Pure Beauty I was searching for. My young student thought (thinks) the same. I arrived (we arrived) in New York with my Study of a Great Papaya and I set about showing it to the Museums, but I only had contact with low-level employees lacking in the classical attributes necessary to Appreciate Art. Then I entered into the world of Galleries. In the ninth one I visited, a blond man whose face was full of tiny moles said that my Work was interesting and we made a deal. He offered to Exhibit the Work to see what would happen. And to "analyze the chemistry," he explained, "that occurred between the Expert Eyes and my interesting Painting Proposal." My beloved young student remained with me and she Admired me and she continued to loan me her lips and her neck in order to keep Inspiration alive. After eleven days, a man wearing a green suit bought my Painting and mentioned that he wanted to Meet me. The man with the tiny moles, my young student, an older Critic, and I ate in an Italian restaurant called The Grand Ticino. Later on we were joined by Yoko Ono. We spoke of Poetry (a bit of William Carlos Williams and a bit of Robert Penn Warren), Art in general (a bit of Rothko and a bit of

Stella), and specifically about the Beauty of my Painting. In the end we agreed that I would Paint another Decomposing Fruit and he would buy the Result (sight unseen, with complete confidence in my Talent) for the sum of two thousand two hundred and fifty dollars. My dear young student set about to make history and obtained a magnificent object for me (a simple tomato). I left it close to the radiator for a few days so it would rot and I Painted it one afternoon during a heavy snowfall. The man with the tiny moles was a bit doubtful when he saw my Work and he called the man in the green suit, who arrived in my Studio (with a tennis player named Nastase and with a musician by the name of Ringo), dressed in a gray suit. He assured me that it was a perfect Tomato and that I had taken an Interesting Step toward my definitive Success. His guests agreed. He handed me a check for four thousand five hundred dollars, having forgotten the amount we had agreed upon, and I took advantage of the situation. That night I went with my young student to the drugstore. She took a pregnancy test and it turned out to be positive. We were both happy and we went to eat everything she craved (a couple of tuna fish hamburgers, potato chips in a bag, and apple pie, a total of $18.75). The following day a woman named Gertrudis called and said she wanted to do an Interview with me for TV. We agreed to meet at the subway entrance and then look for a place which would go with the type of questions that I would authorize her to ask. Instead of interviewing me she told me right out, there on Mercer and Prince, that she wanted to handle my Case. I didn't know at that time what my Case was. She explained that without a good lawyer they would take much of what I had rightfully coming to me. I agreed to her offer and, as she had a good body, I kissed her on her neck, but she got embarrassed as people were looking at us. Back at the Studio, I told the mother of my future child absolutely everything and she responded that since I was a Great Artist I could do Anything I so Desired. I was quite pleased and I started to Paint a head of spinach, the only thing in the refrigerator. The Painting wound up being so poorly executed that I didn't dare to show it to my significant Other. (I even thought I was being visited by that Torpor which was also plaguing the Talented Lichtenstein.) Until one day the young student found it hidden behind the oven. She told me, with her characteristic simplicity (and not without reason) that it was Marvelous. Her words Rekindled my Spirit. Feeling at peace with Myself, I brought my Work to the man with the tiny moles, he brought it to the man in the green or gray suit who greatly Respected me, and in the end a woman named Marguerite, a respected Collector who was very short, bought the work. The mother of my future child, the young student who for so long had allowed me to cover her in kisses and to eventually conceive with her, whose name is Elena, accompanied me to the theater and then ate dinner with me in a place where Artists ate. She ordered lamb chops with mint jelly and I ordered the same. Along with the dinner we drank a wine that tasted slightly of squid or octopus. Pavorotti looked over at us and we toasted from a distance. Truman Capote tried to Recognize me from a distant table. I'm not sure he ever did. Later, a fat, gray-haired, completely bald man around fifty or sixty years old named Bob asked if I was the Painter of the Papaya. Wonderful Elena told him right away that I was. The gentleman sat at our table and Flattered me for close to a quarter of an hour. He told me that mine was the only Avant-Garde without recognizable influences in the History of World Art. And he was right. We spoke of modern Beauty, of the poor novels of poor Philip, of the overabundance of Art in our time, of Genius Hopper and the No Less Genius Rauschenberg. He paid our bill ($98.15) and told me he wanted to do business with Me. I thought the idea was fabulous and I invited him to take a walk the following day along the lovely streets of the Village. We met in a used record store that we both knew and respected. Carrying a couple of pastries ($2.00), we began to Walk and make History. (When one is aware that one is making History, one tries to be Lucid.) He explained to me in no uncertain terms that the man in the green or gray suit wasn't to be trusted, that he had already shaken down many others (such as the unavoidable Pollock). Because of his words and sincere revelations I decided to place myself in his expert hands. As we were saying good-bye, Leonard Bernstein came up to us. Fat Bob told him I was the painter of the Papaya and the Genius Composer gave me a sincere kiss on the Hand. Embarrassment. I tried to return his humble gesture, as I admired him too, but he wouldn't have it. Uncertainty. At nine o'clock Elena gave birth to our child, who turned out very Well, and we named him Jasper, for that was the name of his grandfather on his mother's side (a politician) and on his father's side (a Gnostic). My Unbounded Emotion, Inspiration, and Desire were such that I began to Do Things, like Paint a truly great Mandarin Orange in the hospital room. The lovely lawyer with an attractive body, Gertrudis (who brought as a gift a little green jumpsuit), suggested that I leave my Mandarin Orange in her professional hands so that she could give it its Deserved Place in the Art World. Bob (who brought a yellow jumpsuit) respectfully asked me to tell him what amount he should put on the check in order to make my Latest Work his (I asked for ten thousand Symbolic dollars). The blond man with the tiny moles (who came with a dozen little white shirts) promised me a Retrospective of my work in the Museum. And Marguerite, who I found out was the

French lover of the man in the green and gray suits, came to our house with a pot full of *romeritos*.* It had been such a long time since Elena and I had eaten *romeritos* that I wound up accepting her offer of selling the story of my life to a Famous film producer. It took me a long time to Remember my Story, to tell it to a man named Crock, and to be present during Francis's filming. When I saw that a Lovely Young Woman named Foster was to play the part (in the Film) of the Elena I knew and had an Tremendous Son with, I felt uncomfortable with Myself (played by a very well-known actor whose name I forget). One afternoon, when they were shooting my kissing sessions with Elena, Miss Foster noticed that I felt Weird, and she asked that I accompany her to her dressing room. I went with her and she made Love to me (much to my Surprise). I was fascinated playing with her silky hair and breathing in her breath. Back home, with the much-missed Jasper at My side, for whom I had bought an electric train in a specialty store, I began to do What I do Best. I sketched a still life with the fruit and vegetables I found in the refrigerator. Elena asked me if I had slept with Foster. I've always believed that women can tell when a man has slept with an actress. I answered her objectively and she gave me a hug and tried to give me a kiss on my Neck. I

---

*a typical Mexican dish widely consumed during Easter

swear that if I had had the Urge to continue the little game I would have, but it wasn't so and she wound up being a little disappointed with my Attitude. We stared into each other's eyes for a while, until I looked away and asked if there was anything interesting on TV. As if she hadn't heard what I said, she asked for a divorce. That was quite rough for Me, and I went through really Horrifying moments because of it. All because Jasper loved me and I loved him. After many arguments, I accepted Elena's proposal of ending our relationship the day my Movie was first shown. As part of our civilized breakup, we went to the Premier together. The Success among the People in the Know was so great that Elena kissed me all over (in the movie theater's bathroom) and we got back together and I painted a Melon that very night. On the answering machine there were messages from Malulis, Sylvester, Beuys, Nancy, and Tom Wolfe, who was hoping to Interview me. Marguerite came to see me the next day and stood in front of my Great Melon. She told me that I had gone too far, I had created the Truly Perfect Work, that my Melon (she said this to me in all sincerity) was an Absolutely Beautiful, Fabulous Melon. She immediately proposed to Exhibit it in the Museum so that all Humanity could appreciate it before she took it away to one of her mansions (probably the one in Idaho), in exchange for the seventy-eight thousand, two hundred and fifty dollars she was offering me. The day of the Exhibition was Glorious. DeKooning gave me a big hug, Estes invited me to his house, and Christo was thinking of wrapping my Creation. Woody Allen, in his own inimitable style, spoke to me about the melons he had tried to film all his Great Life, while Warhol suggested that one should distance themselves a bit from the Work in order to Appreciate it. Dustin Hoffman didn't even bother to say hello. According to one of my assistants, he was preoccupied. The Critics admired the Melon, the General Public was wowed by it, a Secretary of State assured me that we had met in Peggy's house and that the following morning the wives or lovers of Prominent Businessmen would be calling me at all hours (without bothering to think that I, too, Sleep). Ink flowed freely in the newspapers and specialized magazines and, as they say, a bit of Art History was made. Even Jasper found out when one of his teachers explained to his mathematics class that his father (I) had managed to create with his own Hands what is now crudely known as Nonobjectionable Art. One day, Elena got fed up with so many phone calls. "Your Fame is beginning to bother me." She threw a carrot cake that she had baked with her own lovely brown hands into my face. I cleaned myself off with a green towel and realized that the moment had come in which to begin a new Life, one beyond Art. Like Vincent the Great. I bought a Gun from a policeman ($850).

damn kids

I'M A DAMN KID. I KNOW IT BECAUSE EVERYONE TELLS me so. Stop that, you damn kid. Leave that alone, you damn kid. What are you doing, you damn kid. I get this every day, from just about everyone. The truth is, the things I do are what any damn kid would do. I know that.

One day I decided to kill flies. I killed seventy-two and collected them in a plastic bag. Everyone was grossed out, even though I was careful not to squash them and stain the walls. I only splattered one of them, the fattest one of all, but then I cleaned it up. I guess the fact that I picked them up with my hands is what bothered my family the most. The truth is, the flies were the real bother. My mother used to say, Damn flies. My father said, Damn heat. I can't take these flies any more. Damn life. So one day I said, I'm going to kill them. No one told me not to do it. As soon as my parents went to take their nap, I grabbed a flyswatter and killed seventy-two. Concha saw me grabbing the dead flies with my hand and putting them in the plastic bag. She told my parents. Instead of thanking me they said, Damn kid, you're disgusting. And they took away the flyswatter and threw the plastic bag in the trash and then told me, Damn kid, you're a devil child.

I already knew by that time that what I was doing was what all damn kids do. Like Rodrigo. Rodrigo pulled all the petals off of the roses the family had given to his mother when she had an operation, and they called him a damn kid. They even gave him a beating, I think. And Mariana, who stole a newborn kitten from Apartment 2 and put it into a micro-wave oven, they called her a damn kid.

We damn kids got together from time to time in the building's garden. It's not like we made a con-scious effort to be damn kids. It's just that there was something inside of us that made us like that, there was nothing we could do about it. For example, one day Mariana decided to excavate. The three of us excavated the entire day. We didn't find any trea-sure, any unusual rocks for our collection, or even any worms. We found bones. Rodrigo's father said, Damn hole. His mother said, They're bones. The police came and said they were human bones. I don't know exactly what happened, but Mariana's mother disappeared for a few days. Concha told me she was in jail. Rodrigo heard his father say that she had killed someone and buried them there. When she returned, we learned that we were all a bunch of nosy bastard damn kids. Rodrigo cleared things up for me. He told me the police thought she had killed someone but in fact she hadn't, and so she was saved from the joint. What's the joint, I asked. Jail, you idiot.

We never excavated again, and we weren't allowed to see each other for a while. My parents told me I shouldn't hang out with them. The others were told the same, and that I was an unruly lying damn kid. Rodrigo's parents whacked him with the belt a few times.

Sometime later, when no one cared that us damn kids got together again, Mariana had the idea that we should excavate some more. No, didn't you see what almost happened to your mother? Nothing happened, remember? We kept guard to make sure no one saw us. We started excavating in one spot but we didn't find any bones, so we dug somewhere else. There weren't any bones there, either, but we did find one bit of treasure. A gun. It must be worth a lot. A real lot, I'd say. Maybe it was the one used to kill the guy in the hole. Maybe. Yeah, we should sell it.

We hid the gun in the room where the gardener kept his stuff. Rodrigo said he knew how to use a gun. My Daddy has one and he lets me use it when we go to Pachuca. Mariana didn't believe him, That's what happens when you watch too much television.

The next day we took the gun out again and wrapped it up in newspaper. How are we going to sell it? Who are we going to sell it to? Mr. Miranda, the guy who owns the store. We went to see Mr. Miranda and he stared at us with his eyes bugging out. Then he told us he was going to buy it, but only because he liked us. Yeah, yeah. Okay. But nobody must know, okay? He gave us a box of chewing gum and fifty pesos. We spent the rest of the afternoon chewing gum until we finished off the box.

The next week, the whole neighborhood knew that Mr. Miranda had a gun. Truth is, I didn't tell anyone, except for Concha. And the only thing she could think of saying was, Damn kid, you're making it up. You're just saying that. It's your imagination. Until one day Mr. Miranda called us and said, Enough already, you damn kids. Stop spreading rumors and do something else with your spare time. Go out and play. He gave us three ice-cream cones so we would stop fucking with him.

At that time, to keep from being bored, we collected snails. We liked to throw them off the roof, or sprinkle salt on them to watch them melt, or stick them in mailboxes. Soon, it was impossible to find a single snail in the whole garden, so we decided to start collecting odd rocks, until someone threw our collection into the garbage. Or stole it, just like that.

THAT'S when we decided to run away. It was Mariana's idea.

I put my jacket on and grabbed my allowance, which wasn't very much at all, since Concha takes money from me when she doesn't have enough to pay the bills. Mariana came out with her jacket and her father's wallet. We gotta split, she said. If they find out they're gonna grab us. Rodrigo didn't bring anything.

We walked about an hour until we arrived at a plaza that none of us had seen before. Now what? asked Rodrigo. Let's take a rest, I said. I'm hungry. So am I. Let's go into a restaurant. Is there one around here? We could ask that man. Mister, do you know where there's a restaurant? On that corner, can't you see?

It was a small restaurant. Rodrigo told us that he had gone to many restaurants in his life. The menu, he said to the waiter. We asked for three hamburgers and three Cokes. Who's going to pay? the waiter asked. Me, said Mariana, and she took out her father's wallet. Okay. We heard him say to the cook, Damn kids, they must be good thieves.

He served us three hamburgers and three Cokes. We ate. Mariana paid.

Now what do we do? Shut up, Mariana told me. By now, my father must have found out that his wallet is missing. Are you worried? Why should I be, we've run away, haven't we? Yes. So now what do we do?

Let's go talk to Mr. Miranda.

Rodrigo flagged down a cab. Take us to Calle Argentina. Who's going to pay? Mariana showed him the wallet. Damn kids, you stole the money from your parents, right? Are you going to take us there or not? Rodrigo asked. It's your money, he said.

The taxi driver took us a few blocks to a deserted street. Now, give me the money. No, what're you going to do about it? Look, you damn kids, either give me the money or I'll kill you all. It's ours. I'm going to steal it from you like you stole it from them, okay? And your allowance, too, he said to me. I gave him my allowance. That's right, you damn kids. Now get out.

Fuckin' guy, Mariana said. If I had a gun, I'd a shot him, Rodrigo said. Just like that. I'd like to strangle him. Without money we can't stay in a hotel. I've stayed in lots of hotels, Rodrigo said. But without money . . . Why don't we go to see Mr. Miranda and ask for our gun back? Yeah, that's it. The gun. Then let's see who'll try to rob us.

A man told us how to get to Calle Argentina, and then asked if we were lost. Yes, a little lost. Just go straight, straight to Dominguez, then take a left, got that? Do you know which street is Dominguez? I didn't know, but Mariana said she did. Truth is, the man was very nice.

To make a long story short, when we finally got to Mr. Miranda's store it was already night. Now what do you want? he asked. I'm about to close up. We want the gun. Yeah, and we want to buy some ammo. Look, you damn kids, I told you to stop spreading rumors. Here's some chewing gum and now beat it. No, we just want the gun, that's all. I'm closing, get out of here. And you can forget about the chewing gum.

Rodrigo grabbed a bag of flour, opened it up and threw a fistful into poor Mr. Miranda's eyes. Damn kids, your parents are going to get you for this. The old man fell to the floor. I jumped onto his head and started to pull his hair. Meanwhile, Mariana was pinching his arm as hard as she could. Go find the gun, hurry up, we said to Rodrigo. Where? Down there. No, it's not there. Then over there, next to the cash register. Get off of me you damn kids, he yelled. No, it's not here, either. Where is it, you damn old man? If you don't get off of me . . . Here it is, Rodrigo yelled, here it is. Where was it? In the cash register.

Now what. Do we kill him? Mariana was grabbing Mr. Miranda's legs so he couldn't move. See if it has any bullets. Yep, it has bullets. Should we fill him with lead. Fill him with lead? Kill him, you idiot. Yeah, kill him. Damn kids . . .

The noise of the gunshot was frightening, I never knew a gun was so loud. A stream of blood poured out of poor Mr. Miranda's head and he lay there dead. Is he dead? Of course, can't you tell? You see, I do know how to shoot a gun. Fuck, Mariana said. Yeah, fuck.

Let's go before someone comes. We went straight ahead along Argentina, running as fast as we could, until we came to Rodrigo's school. A lady bumped into Mariana. She said, Damn kid, watch where you're going.

I don't know how he did it, but Rodrigo pulled the gun out lightning fast and shot her in the belly. The woman fell to the ground and started to scream. She's not dead yet, I said, you'll have to give her some more lead. Rodrigo shot her in the head.

Now she is, Mariana proclaimed. She's iced. You touched her? She's dead, you idiot.

It seems that others had heard the gunshot because people started to crowd in around the body. Rodrigo had already put the gun back into his jacket pocket.

Call an ambulance! Call the police! Call someone! She's been murdered! I think she's been shot. Has anyone taken her pulse? I heard it all. I ran out of my house to see what happened and I saw . . . I saw a man running away. He had a gun in his hand. You should testify. Of course, as soon as the police get here. She's not breathing. Get out of the way, you damn kids, can't you see she's dead. No one's safe in this neighborhood. It's fucking dangerous. Did they steal her bag? Yeah, I saw the man running with a gun and the lady's bag. It was a white bag. Didn't you hear what I said, you damn nosy kids. If your parents saw you here. There were two guys, they had guns and they were carrying her bag. I know her, it's Mariquita, Gustavo's wife. He's going to be really upset.

When we heard the sirens coming close, Mariana said we should go before there was trouble.

We shouldn't have killed her, I said as we walked toward the avenue. It was her fault. That's just how things are, lots of people are killed like that. In the street, with a gun. You shouldn't worry, they say that you go right to Heaven if you're shot to death. Yeah, that's true, I've heard that before. Do you think that Mr. Miranda'll also go to Heaven? Of course, you moron.

Mariana hailed a taxi. Where are we going? We don't have any money to pay for the ride. Don't be so naive, she said. Take us to Calle Lopez, Rodrigo said. Which Calle Lopez? Do you know what time it is? No, I said to him. It's ten o'clock. Are you going to take us there or not? Mariana said. Look, you damn kids, if your parents let you take taxis this late at night it's your problem, but I won't, so just get out, get out of here. Rodrigo pulled the gun out and pointed it at the man's face. Damn kid, I'm going to give you a beating for fucking with me.

When he went to grab the pistol, Rodrigo shot him. The bullet went right through his eye. We sent him right to Heaven, without a doubt.

I know how to drive, Rodrigo said, but it wasn't true. When we finally pushed the taxi driver to one side, Rodrigo tried to get the cab started but he couldn't. Put it into first. I know, I know. Let me do it, Mariana said. She sat behind the wheel, put it into first, and the car moved a little bit, jolting forward and backward. Let's walk instead, I said. Yeah, this car doesn't work very well.

Before leaving the taxi, Rodrigo went through the driver's pockets until he found money. There's more than a hundred pesos. Take his watch, too. We'll sell it later. Mariana put the money into her pocket, I put the watch on and Rodrigo hid the gun in his jacket.

In the hotel it was the same hassle. Where are your parents, do you know what time it is, a hotel isn't for kids to play in, renting a room isn't for free, where's the money. Go fuck yourself, Rodrigo said, and we all ran out.

We walked a little while until Mariana had an idea. I know, we can sleep at Mrs. Ana Dulce's house. With that old bag? Yeah, you idiot, we sneak into her house, fill her with lead and spend the night there. Shit, that is a good idea.

Mrs. Ana Dulce opened the door. What do you want? Can we use your telephone? we said in order to throw her off the track. Damn kids, do you know what time it is? We went into the house without paying any attention to the old woman's threats. I'm going to call the police and tell them you've run away from home. Then you'll see what kind of a beating you'll get. I saw Mariana arguing with Rodrigo. It's my turn. But you don't know how. Mariana apparently won because she took the gun and shot Mrs. Ana Dulce. She hit her in her foot. Then she shot her again. How about that one, she said. I bet you I hit her in her heart. I was thinking the same, even though the old bag was howling in pain like a madwoman and rolling around on the floor. She shut up after a while.

We'll hide her in the closet. Rodrigo called her a corpse. Then we ate bread and butter and marmalade and the three of us went into bed together with the gun under the pillow. During the next ten days we didn't shoot anyone else. There was only one bullet left. We went to the park every morning and ate and slept in the corpse's house, until the horrible smell coming from the closet made us run out of there.

That day we had the bad luck of running right smack into Mariana's dad. Damn kids, he shouted! We've looked everywhere for you! Now you'll see what you've got coming!

We couldn't have imagined what was waiting for us. They kicked us and whipped us and slapped us and stomped on us. I heard Mariana and Rodrigo yelling. My mother smacked me in the face and blood came out of my nose, and my father back-handed me in the mouth and almost knocked one of

21

my teeth out. No matter how much I cried, they kept hitting me and hitting me, like a dog.

It took a while for me to fall asleep. But a little while later I was awakened by a gunshot. Rodrigo must have knocked off his parents, I thought. Then I heard shouts. My parents also woke up and ran to the door to see what was happening.

Rodrigo's mother was yelling, He killed him, he killed him, he killed him! The damn kid killed him! Calm down, lady. Who killed who? At that moment, Rodrigo came out with the gun in his hand. Run, before they grab us. This is war. And Mariana, I asked? We have to get her. No, just run.

And so we ran the fuck out of there. We were really glad to run into our friend on the street. He took out his parents, I announced. Fuck, Mariana said, that's what I thought. And we started to run as if a pack of wild dogs were after us. We didn't stop until Rodrigo tripped on a rock and hit the ground. Blood poured from his nose.

I really fucked myself up, he said, a bit dazed and confused. And in fact he really had fucked himself up. I could even see a little bit of bone sticking out.

THE three of us were wearing our pajamas and the two of them were barefoot. I was the only one wearing socks. Could you lend them to me for a while? Mariana asked. It's very cold. I lent them to her.

So now what do we do? There's no way I'm going back to the corpse's house. We still have the gun, don't we? We could knock on someone's door and kill whoever answers. Don't be an idiot, that's fucking crazy. Besides, we're out of bullets. How could you think that anyone's going to open their door for us? That's true, we're a bunch of murderers. That's not why.

It was so cold I wanted to take a piss. I half pissed my underwear and the rest went onto the wheel of a car. Damn pig, Mariana said. Rodrigo burst out laughing.

We walked a little way until we came to a house with broken windows. It must be abandoned. Sure. We broke one of the windows and climbed in. It was completely dark.

We found a room that let in a little bit of light from the street. We pushed the garbage to one side and lay down on the floor, as close as possible to keep each other warm, until we fell asleep. Until we finally fell asleep.

THE next morning, my bones aching, I woke up the others. Now we could see what the room we had slept in was like. It was wet and dirty. There were empty beer cans, cigarette butts, plastic bags, orange peels, and mounds of dirt. It smelled like shit.

Mariana was shivering and burning hot at the same time. She must have a fever, I said. A fever so bad we should call a doctor. A doctor, Rodrigo said, angry. How do you feel, I asked her? She didn't even answer me. Just shivered and shivered.

We have to buy aspirin. That's true, I said. Rodrigo offered to look for a drugstore while I took care of Mariana.

We waited for hours and hours, until finally Mariana stopped shaking. When she told me she felt better I explained that Rodrigo had gone to look for a drugstore to buy aspirins and that he still hadn't come back yet. He's late. Of course he's late. Something must have happened to him.

We looked and looked for him until we got lost and we no longer knew how to go back to the house where we had slept. We were incredibly hungry. Without money. Without the gun. Without a house where we would be fed.

The rest was Mariana's idea. We begged money from cars at a stoplight. When we had filled up our pockets with change we sat down to count it. Nine pesos and twenty centavos. We went to a store and bought two bags of potato chips and two sodas.

After eating we lay down on the grass on the traffic island. We talked about Rodrigo for a long time. What happened to him? Who knows? Did the police nab him for killing his parents? Or maybe he was just lost. Like us. Or maybe they grabbed him when he tried to kill the guy in the drugstore. But he had no bullets. Or else he got hit by a car. Who knows? Or they shot him for being nosy.

Night came and we had nowhere to sleep. We had no choice but to ask someone where Calle Lopez was and go to the house of Mrs. Ana Dulce. Even though it smelled ugly, at least there'd be a bed there.

It took us about two hours to get there. Outside Mrs. Ana Dulce's house was a cop. I think maybe . . . Yeah, yeah, you don't have to spell it out. What do we do? Shit, you got me.

We slept in an empty lot full of rats. I'm goddamned sure of it. We spent a completely fucked-up night.

We woke up wet and our chests were frozen solid. We were terribly hungry. What if we go home? What did you say? Rodrigo killed his father. Rodrigo is Rodrigo. He might even be dead by now.

Concha was the first to see us: Damn kids, just wait and see what's going to happen to you.

AND she was right about what was going to happen to us. . . . But with Mariana's character, they never imagined what was in store for them.

the war, this time, was getting serious

THE WAR, THIS TIME, WAS GETTING SERIOUS. WE realized it when Manuel was shot in his lumbar region. Immediately after, flaming arrows and gasoline-filled balloons came flying through the window. The unsuspected nature of the attack made Javier curse, and we were forced to end our third birthday party for Julia, a delicious dinner that consisted of smoked herring, ribs, green cabbage, and toast.

We decided not to shut the windows, since we considered it a wasted effort—they would just be smashed anyway. We limited ourselves to putting out the small fires that broke out in the living room, the dining room, and the bedrooms, and we avoided the aggresive little blasts of lead our enemies' fury launched at us. Only Julia had fun: she made stacks of broken glass and bullet casings, and built a city with them beneath the dinner table. Manuel also tried to find a safe spot within the war. He erected a barricade in front of the window from which he would peek out from time to time, laughing and winking at the snipers, protected by his shining shield of gilded plastic.

Laura couldn't restrain her anger at the interruption of the dinner. She finished cleaning up the table and spat out the name of the one she had chosen to be her victim. We tried to convince her that it wasn't necessary to hurt anyone, that vengeance wasn't called for since there hadn't yet been any casualties within our family, that we had to be humane toward our adversaries as long as possible. But our reasoning and entreaties were to no avail. Laura said not a word, and she headed out into the street with vengeance in her heart.

The war did indeed seem to be getting serious. At least more serious than at other times. The Millán clan were hell-bent on exterminating us in any way they could. Their faces behind the bows and rifles were swollen with anger, frustrated at their inability to send off a thousand rounds of ammunition with a single squeeze of the trigger, a thousand flaming arrows with a single shot of the bow, at their inability to convert our apartment into a conflagration that would erase the last evidence of our obviously superior spirituality.

In both buildings, the Milláns' and ours, the neighbors were poking their heads out of windows.

They knew that only an accident, a very improbable one given the marksmanship of the Milláns, would set fire to their apartments. No one turned on any lights, for the spectacle of the flaming arrows crossing in the night from building to building was Olympic, spellbinding. In order to liven up the event and give a touch of class and hospitality to our viewing public, Manuel put on a Rossini record at full volume, with rifle retorts and Julia's enthusiastic shouts serving as counterpoint.

While he was savoring a herring, Javier was hit in the leg, which he rubbed delicately. At that moment Laura returned, smiling from ear to ear. She went directly to her room and, transfigured by glee, raised one of the venetian blinds to watch the stupified face of Esteban Millán at the precise moment that a blast lit up the street. His Volkswagen.

Just before the sun came up the battle reached its end. The Milláns' arsenal had been depleted long before their anger and our patience. In a fit of frustration, Ulíses, the patriarch and commanding officer of our enemy, wound up throwing the glass in which he drank his habitual aged rum at us. These were the last shards that Julia rescued for her construction.

The living room was left rank and humid. Broken mirrors, black stains on the carpet and couches, a barricade of punctured pillows, a half-eaten herring, a haphazard crystal city beneath the table.

One day, weeks later, the Milláns died.

Only one of them survived, Martín, the most hateful. At the funeral, in front of the depressing scene of the four caskets, he swore vengeance. The Gallos, his faithful in-laws, offered him their support, especially Refugio, his wife, the most hateful (of the Gallos).

We found out that they were getting together in the afternoons to prepare the details of their much-announced revenge. Nonetheless, weeks went by without the slightest sign of the promised attack. Just when we had begun to stop worrying, we received a call from Texas. Laura's lake, or rather her trout, had been dynamited. An hour later we received another call. Manuel's car repair shop, which had been so difficult for him to acquire, was being attended to by firemen.

We never knew why Javier's restaurant, Cheto's Grill, had escaped the enemy's grasp. The truth is, given the amount of time they had taken to make their move, the losses were almost insignificant. Once again, we decided to maintain silence. Except for Laura, who did something on her own and without telling us about it. She called up Refugio and talked to her about death in warm, beautiful, and convincing phrases. Glorious death.

A HALF-HOUR later, Refugio Gallo de Millán shot and killed herself with a pistol.

30

People at her wake showed the grief appropriate to such an event. The family consoled each other for the unforgettable loss, and they mourned over the senseless act. Especially her father, the most humane of the Gallos. A craving for revenge overtook the widowed Martín; it was so uncontrollable that, not knowing what to do with his hands and without realizing it, he threw Tobi, the Milláns' small Pekingese dog who had been a companion to Refugio for years, out the window.

Martín and the Gallos redoubled their promises of vengeance, accompanied by the blaring music that Manuel had thoughtfully put on the stereo: "The Niebelungen."

And so it happened that, days later, Martín knocked on our door to announce the plans that they had decided upon. Never before had he been so elegantly dressed and carefully groomed. He wore a shiny tuxedo, leather gloves, golden cufflinks, a world-famous cologne, and patent leather shoes, and he carried a silver-handled cane. We invited him in to have some tea and to discuss the details of the operations. He informed us, in seventeenth-century phrasing that Javier quickly identified, that the next battle would be the last and that his combative mind had plotted out a war between the two buildings, having already asked his neighbors to participate. He informed us that the date, which was not negotiable, would be the following Sunday. Eight A.M.

He took his leave of us, wished us well and, with a sporting air, he wished us luck in the contest. Before he left he threatened Laura, telling her that next Sunday they would grab her and throw her out the window in the midst of all her allies. At Manuel he only winked; it was undoubtedly a sign.

Laura was horrified at the thought of her body becoming a stamp, a sticker on the oily surface of the sidewalk. The scent of pine trees that had characterized her among the upper circles of Texan entrepreneurs dissipated, and in its place she was surrounded by the bitter breath of death. Glorious death in the shape of a cream puff smashed on her native earth.

WHILE Javier patiently studied British strategy from the Second World War in the library, Laura was in charge of recruiting the neighbors, all of whom gladly agreed. There was barely time to get organized and to buy the necessary provisions and weapons. Friday was to be the Front's final counsel, Saturday practice and simulations, and Sunday the much-awaited clash.

Almost everyone arrived at the meeting on Friday an hour early, with offensive and defensive plans in writing. Some came dressed in military uniforms, while several kids wore well-ironed Superman, Robin Hood, and D'Artagnan outfits. The film critic from 201 came in carrying a huge stone on his shoulders, with a burning torch in his hand. It was quite moving to see the enthusiasm and activity of all the comrades from the building.

The actress from 609 offered to get a police permit to close the street off from traffic for the appointed day. The cavalryman from 1003, Commander Tor, said he had managed to get a bazooka which, as a favor to Javier, would only be used as a final solution. Without previous consultation, the tailor from 701 bought one million pins and needles without really knowing how they could possibly be used. The sandpaper manufacturer from 909 offered to distribute drills, screwdrivers, nails, hammers, pliers, saws, and several varieties of sandpaper to all the neighbors the following day. One kid, no less enthusiatic than the adults, offered up his slingshot, an offer that produced a round, clear, emotional tear from Javier.

NIGHT began to fade into the first light of the morning when Javier, with the use of a loudspeaker, summed up the ideas proposed by the members of the Front and set the strategy to be followed. Once the orders were fully outlined, Manuel offered a touch of elegance and class, so characteristic of him. Before the attack began, all the stereos in the building would simultaneously play Ravel. For this purpose, Manuel had bought several dozen "Boleros," which he handed out amid an outpouring of good cheer.

On the day before the event, before the simulations began, Laura checked out all the installations. The apartment of the orthodontist in 102 was set up as a hospital, of which the gynecologist from 108 was put in charge. Javier had bought bandages, alcohol, syringes, capsules, and adult and children's aspirin. The living room of the acupuncturist in 305 was set up as a mess hall, in case the war should continue longer than planned, or in case someone got hungry. For this purpose, lots of canned goods and sausages, eggs, sodas, toast, peaches, herbs and spices (of which Laura was a fan, especially dill), and a few pounds of smoked herring (for Javier) had been purchased.

Several people not from the building who had found out about the war called to offer their services. At first Manuel accepted them, wrote their names down on the list and gave them instructions. Then, as the number of volunteers grew, and fearing the advent of a catastrophe, he rejected them in a friendly way. The rooftops were already set up for some forty allied sharpshooters.

An army general, a friend of the surveyor in 1114, offered to place a battalion and a tank in the surrounding streets. Javier, as calm as a magazine in a doctor's waiting room, convinced him to desist. For their part, the union of public announcers, who had already given the war so much publicity, offered to bring together a group of commandos made up of fearless men to set fire to the enemy's building. This time it was Laura who had to convince the leader that this was to be a private war.

After Saturday's simulations and preparations, held secretly in a baseball park in the outskirts of the city, we offered a ceremonial toast of wine to everyone, to show our profound appreciation.

SATURDAY, midnight. Manuel, not wanting to take any risks, organized a general rehearsal of the background music. In a frock coat and with a baton in his hand, he stepped out onto the balcony and shot off a Roman candle. "Bolero" exploded in unison. Although the Cyprian from 505 lagged behind, Javier, who for years had studied synchronicity from a metaphysical perspective, approved of the harmonic unity with a slight movement of his index finger.

The lights came on in Martín's apartment. We watched as he looked out the window, surprised at what he must have seen as a sign of reconciliation. Manuel saw to it that he was disabused of this idea with the same symbolic gesture that days before Martín had used as a threat: he winked at him.

SUNDAY, 8 A.M. A cool breeze, a slight birdsong, and suddenly Ravel's "Bolero" flooded through the building, the street, the whole neighborhood. A trumpet blast from the twelfth floor and armed people immediately began to vomit forth from the entrance to the urban Trojan Horse. Our opponents came out a few moments later, dressed in showy yellow uniforms, rose-colored berets, and silver shields. They began shooting gasoline-filled balloons and flaming arrows, the favorite weapons of the pyromaniac Martín. Streams of ammunition and large quantities of ice poured out from different floors. One notoriously crazy woman showered the swarm of people in the street with nitric acid. Meanwhile, the bullfighter from 306 gave the veterinarian from 703 the opportunity to professionally kill the young bull our enemies had let loose in the street. He only took a single ear as a trophy.

In the meantime, Martín skillfully shot marbles at the skulls of his enemy. Laura got hit by one on the chin. She immediately sent it back with all her force toward the window where Martín was laughing, but since he ducked in time, the marble landed in the bathroom. His most costly cologne spilled onto the floor. Martín wept.

The children poked one another in the eyes and bit each other. One of them, disguised as a praline, licked and drooled on the wounded. It was quite unpleasant to watch. Javier had to give him a smack, to the amusement of his victims. Another boy, dressed as a doctor, tried to sew up the mouth of a wounded old man with needle and thread. Next to them, a little girl spat out nonsense phrases and made obscene gestures to a woman who was praying for peace.

THE battle, which Manuel and I observed from the window with our new pair of binoculars, was developing harmonically. Destruction everywhere. Those who hit were hit in turn. Those who bit were attacked with teeth. Those who burned were burnt. Those who bruised were knocked out. Those who rumored, were belied. Someone lost a tooth and they got it back with the help of the professional services of the orthodontist from 102. Just one eye, staring up like a Greek statue from the asphalt, remained unclaimed, all alone, without its mate.

All kinds of objects and substances rained down from the rooftops and the windows of the highest floors. Live cats, cheap perfume, ink, honey, fistfuls of needles, tartar sauce. Those down below had to quickly find umbrellas and raincoats to protect themselves from the aerial attacks. Some people preferred to undertake individual battles, inviting their enemy to continue the combat under the roof and in the warmth of their own apartments.

In Laura's opinion, people began to go crazy. Even Commander Tor lost control and aimed his bazooka at the crowd of people. Javier had to inject him with a milky substance and then hide the weapon behind the refrigerator. The librarian from 109 also went loony, and in cold blood from the window of the fifth floor, he dumped three small, fragile bunny rabbits that smashed onto the sidewalk.

AT the first chords of the second movement of "Bolero," the smoke from the burning tires in the street barely allowed one to see the outlines of the warriors who still remained standing. We saw two old men with long silver-fox curls beat each other while a young student, right next to them, read aloud from the *Paideia* to a healthy group of women. We could distinguish in several different points within the bellicose spectacle several bodies lying beside fires, garbage, dead cats. It was a horrible picture, comparable to certain films that aren't worth remembering. An authentic spiritual dunghill. The world's great stage in which, instead of applauding the great performance, one reaches for the antidepressants.

Which is just what Manuel did. He ate three. But he soon realized that this was in vain, as the effects would take too long, and that the depression that was creeping up on him with dark feelers could be halted neither by a double session of psychoanalysis nor by his favorite television program. It was something disastrous, inconceivable, final. The frightening reality that was the world. He thought up a phrase, which he whispered in my ear so I would jot it down in his diary: "Man is the wolf's wolf." He couldn't take it anymore. His soul was dessicated, destroyed, an insignificant gust of air. He had to find the strength somewhere to confront that hornets' nest battling in front of his eyes, fighting just to fight.

From within his shelter, a tent located in the center of the battle, Javier, as human as ever and as in control of the situation as ever, reflected. His thoughts led him to conceive of a final point, an irrevocable, infallible peace treaty.

Finally, Manuel decided to step out determinedly onto his balcony and to yell with all the air in his lungs: "Silence, impoverished humanity." Even the "Bolero," in response to the voice and the sentiments of the young leader, had to accelerate the last notes of the second movement to almost fifty revolutions per minute in order to give way to the asked-for silence. Javier seconded him with equal disgust and without any less volume: "Halt, ye empty men."

A heavy silence ensued. The onlookers of our war, stationed on the rooftops of the nearby buildings, in helicopters, blimps, and on traffic islands and streetlights, were caught so unaware by Manuel's forceful shout and by Javier's emotional and definitive order that they dared not even whisper. The television cameras fixed their lenses on the expectant multitude, and the newspaper photographers endlessly opened and closed the shutters of their Nikons on the flustered faces of the ex-combatants.

RAVEL offered up the first notes of the third movement to underscore Manuel's salute from the balcony. The applause and shouts instantly exploded. Laura and Julia soon joined in with vibrant cheers, then I, in my rabbit disguise. Silly but sincere chants.

It was Manuel who, with his disconcerting calm, a native of the mountains, addressed the multitudes.

"My dear fellow condominium owners, dear neighbors, dear enemies that are here with us. Let us not stain the river with our blood."

"Oh," shouted the crowd. "Let us not stain it, let us not stain it with our blood."

"That is what I ask of you," Manuel continued. "Let us hold hands as a sign of friendship and let us think of the future marriages and affairs that those of us who are gathered here will one day celebrate."

"Yay!" responded the multitude in chorus. "Let us love each other, let us love each other, let us love each other."

"And," Laura added without any hard feelings, "let us give Martín our forgiveness."

"Yeeeehah!" shouted everyone, as they joined hands and lips and began pairing off in couples and as lovers.

Javier did not bother to offer up words or impose his presence on the balcony, for he had always been a man of action. Amid the applause of the community, he ran toward Martín's apartment and in a few minutes returned with him, arm in arm and full of tears.

The accused asked for forgiveness by means of a loudspeaker. Amid the harmonious din of the Yays and Yeeeehahs to be heard from the populace, Martín let fall a pair of crystal tears, as round as bars of soap. He raised his hands toward the sky, the unbounded sky.

Then he answered the reporters' questions.

the creation

GOD SAID, IN HIS INIMITABLE VOICE: "LET THERE BE light." But something went wrong in the pronunciation of the noun, and the result was unexpected. Electric light. And with that came the night, and soon the first blackout. People robbed and murdered, raped beautiful girls, perpetrated assaults and batteries, committed patricides, frightened little old ladies, kidnapped tycoons and, while stuck in traffic jams, plotted horrible plans of vengeance. "Darkness," God said to His inner being, "has brought evil among men."

He had to correct His mistake, a serious one given that the Omnipresent One had committed it. In order to do it, God first wrote down on a piece of paper (oh, divine graphis) his next desire, and then He intoned it with His best pronunciation: "Let there be goodness." And goodness instantly dispelled the oppressive night that had enveloped the world. Though not without a certain lack of subtlety for those who weren't accustomed to humanity: altruism. Young boys helped old ladies cross the street, neighbors offered each other their wives, tyrants collected money for the Red Cross, beggars opened up savings accounts, the army offered to care for babies while their parents went to the movies, people shook hands at every opportunity and exchanged innumerable gifts with their fellow man. In the hospitals, millions of eyes and kidneys were transplanted and countless transfusions were made, in most cases just as a friendly gesture among the donors. The president opted for democracy, and the pope awarded twenty-three dispensations.

Then, not content with the laid-back sweetness of His latest creation, in fact, rather bored with it, God muttered to Himself: "I want something more normal, something like daily life." His command was immediately carried out. People happily flooded the streets, went to their jobs, took the day off, shipped out to other ports, let themselves be operated on in the hospitals, told their children not to confuse liberty with libido, headed into the subway, spoke French, poked around in their nostrils, ate disgusting purées. A wonderful routine enveloped the world.

Time passed slowly, marked by the noise of the textile factories and by the squeal of tires on the street. Until one fine day when God descended to

Earth. Everything was the same, it was as if He were watching a movie He'd seen many times already. It was truly boring. A little disconcerted by the shouting coming from the stands in the soccer stadium, deafened by the cheers, He decided to end once and for all the monotony of daily life. He quickly said, "Let there be loneliness and silence."

The soccer game ended and each of the ex-fans returned to their homes, their attics, or their tranquil places of marriage. Families, religious orders, rotary clubs, architectural firms, polo teams, lovers, academies, and all kinds of associations were disbanded and their ex-members ran to look for a hideaway to live in. Individuals pondered, conceived ideas, meditated, read David Hume, opened their hearts to memories, poked around in the depths of their soul, practiced yoga, became introverted.

God was touched by such order and serenity. He enjoyed the isolation of His creatures because in this way He had moments to Himself, too. And also because He could amuse Himself by spying on people writing in their isolation. He read all the texts He could find: diaries, letters, sonnets, aphorisms, and lampoons. He thus perceived the full depth of pleasure that many people enjoyed alone. At the same time, He became aware of His own joy when He discovered that He, too, had written, almost without being aware of it, an autobiography.

But with the passing years the silence became

unbearable, out-and-out boring. God desperately needed to hear something, even if it were only dialogue between patients and their psychoanalysts. A conversation about the rain or about the price of gas. Whatever. A program of rock on the radio, an inside tip about a job, a diatribe, a secret, a curse. He'd even be content with a poetry reading.

He had to end His disdain and boredom in a single stroke, deliver the ascetic lifestyle a hard, final blow. He cleared His vocal chords and He spoke in a singsong voice: "Let there be celebration." And the festivities began. The extremists suddenly recovered the color in their cheeks, threw their diaries and memoirs into the fire, and began to sing and dance. Different forms of amusement were to be seen all over the world. People laughed hysterically, won dance contests and prizes in gymnastics, played jokes, threw parties, broke open piñatas, consumed alcohol, composed songs, shot targets, ate gourmet cheeses.

God was excited, wide-eyed, soundly satisfied, absorbed in the contemplation of the jubilation that was spreading over the Earth. Yet how He wished at the same time to be human so He could share with his creatures their joy, their avoidance of responsibilities without commitments or worries. To be able to go to a dance, throw darts at balloons, wear a Superman outfit, shoot craps, sing a *ranchera*.

When He became conscious of His digression and remembered His divine condition, however, He was overtaken by sadness. Being the Creator, he could never be one of His creatures. Then, a sudden doubt replaced His longing, a huge doubt, considering the possibility that the Omniscient One would ever have a doubt: "Is this really the role that I should play as the Lord of Creation? A promoter of parties, gaming, and irresponsibility?" The first thing that occurred to Him was to create, once and for all, reality. To teach the world how to tell it like it is, to be silent in the face of that which can't be spoken, to know that a bird doesn't bring the spring.

A new doubt took hold of God. "If it's reality that we're going to have," He said to Himself, "will I be a reality for man? Will My Being have any meaning for them?" Doubt brought Him to depression, and then to anguish. He didn't want to think any more that day. He preferred to get into bed and to forget about His problems, at least for one night. That night, He dreamed that He was riding on a merry-go-round, that He had a human appearance, something like Shirley Temple, one of his favorite creations, and that he was eating pink cotton candy.

When He awoke, slightly dizzy from His ride on the merry-go-round, it took Him a few minutes to realize that it had all been a dream. In the time it took to shake off His torpor and rub the sleep out of His eyes, He was quickly returning to reality. And yes, it was a reality in which He would be excluded. He recalled His sadness of the previous night and

His image of an anguished God. "No," He then said, determined to put an end to such an unpleasant situation.

Thus He ended His decline: "Let faith be born on this Earth." And faith spread throughout the world in a single instant. The human soul was sown with the seed of piety. Many prayed, the guilt-ridden beat themselves on their chests, others made their knees bleed, or meditated, or gave themselves up completely to contrition, penitence, piety, and adoration. Altars, chapels, temples, churches, basilicas, and cathedrals were built, as were asylums, orphanages, convents, and seminaries. People walked around the streets elegantly dressed in bright new habits. Whenever possible, they exchanged symmetrical signs of the cross with their fellow man. Every Sunday at noon, the people came out of their homes and saluted their Creator with little mirrors. Afterward, they cheered Him on and offered up toasts to Him.

God was happier than ever. He was truly impatient waiting for Sundays to see Himself reproduced millions of times in the echo of the human salute. During the week He kept Himself busy blessing communion wafers, sometimes in the churches and other times, getting ahead of Himself, in the bakeries themselves.

Now He was truly the Center of the Universe, the Omnicenter, the Omni-Everything. Why not, then, give Himself a few pleasures? Why not please Himself? Why not create, if create was His verb, what He would have like to have been and had if He were a creature and not the Creator? Why not a pleasant pastime?

He took a gulp of wine by way of confirmation and gave Himself up to His imagination. To think about things, about what would give Him, and possibly His creatures, pleasure. And then He started to create. Barbra Streisand for the screen, the soccer team of Botafogo for sports (although they would lose their first match 0-2), Pascal for philosophy, Los Panchos for music, a strange seventeenth-century painter (of whom not a single work survives) for the arts, a certain Morris for civil engineering. And then pistachios, Scotch-plaid scarves, pirhanas, two novels by Faulkner, ice cubes, a muscle, hair, nobility, and leather binding.

Exhausted, yet satisfied for having created some of His divine pleasures, God was on the verge of tears from so much happiness, which without knowing He had been storing up within Himself over the centuries. His creatures continued to pray at the same time that they enjoyed and shared the new creations. They were happy in their own way. And God noticed how this happiness filled them up. But He also noticed that something was missing, a little something that would take them away a bit from their prayers.

He felt egotistical. He had to give man a gift that would excite them more than ice cubes or Barbra Streisand's smile. He had to compensate them for their obedience. He thought for three days and their nights, until he finally hit upon it. Sex. And as soon as He had thought of it he snapped His fingers and, despite the fact that it was three in the morning in Brussels, He said: "Let there be sex." And sex spread throughout the Earth with great joy on the part of the participants. People flooded the streets in search of a mate. And they had sex. Lovers, automonosexualites, presbyophiles, gynecoists, exhibitionists, zooerasts, fetishists, multiscopophiles, necrophiles, and braid cutters were to be seen everywhere.

Every day, God would spy on man. First He went to the house of his darling Shirley, but she let Him down. Then He directed His gaze into homes, hotels, apartments, beaches, parked cars, pools, trees, all corners that played host to His servants. One day he found a couple that inspired Him to exclaim, before thinking, "They're divine."

During one of His voyeuristic ecstasies He said through his teeth: "Let there be semen." And His divine semen flooded forth. The only trouble was that there was no recipient, no one to beget. Thus God decided to create for Himself a Goddess, an eternal companion.

The work, as expected, was more difficult than that of creating humans. He first had to define the characteristics of His wife. The only models that came to mind were mortals. A combination of Barbra and Shirley. Then He extracted an intangible, divine, omniperfect rib and He created a wife. The result, by all appearances, wasn't bad. In fact, it was very good, divine.

Before He gave Himself up completely to His obligations with Her, He gave His last command: "Let there be a world determined by its own evolution." And despite the vagueness of the order, a world was thus created, with a history, the remains of that history, the suffering of those remains, and with ideals and self-determination.

the broken-down life of a dead man

1. AT ONE TIME, I WAS WALLOWING IN THE MIRE.

2. I realized that drugs had something to do with it.

3. A medium-tall man with a feathered hat in a cantina warned me that it was risky to get mixed up with them. He also told me that jail is jail and not at all a pleasant place.

4. Be that as it may, I soon forgot his words and I dove in.

5. Mrs. González also was stuck in the mud. She invited me over to her ranch and fed me a strange dessert. Then she told me how to get out of the mire.

6. It wasn't all that difficult, but it also wasn't as easy as I had been told.

7. Chesterton, as the man was called, drove me in his fancy car to the landing field.

8. I flew in a funny little plane for five hours, seated next to a pockmarked pilot by the name of Ernesto, a man of great experience.

9. We gave the bags we were carrying to a short guy who didn't give us anything in return. Ernesto explained that this was how things were in the world of drugs. As he was a man of experience and had no problem with it, I had no problem with it.

10. And of course there was no problem. I was paid the money I was promised and I went home with my pockets bulging.

11. The Toad, my son, boasted at school that we were now rich, and he showed off his new bicycle. I had a gold tooth made for him and I bought him a watch and chain.

12. Mother, as we call my wife, set up a taco joint downtown and began to socialize with Mrs. Dominga and her friends, very well-respected people around here. They are always the first people to arrive for communion in the church.

13. One day Chesterton told me there was a new job to be done. As the money I had earned was dwindling away, I accepted and I asked that he send Ernesto too as we had already become friends.

14. Things had changed, though. I was to fly in a commercial plane and pass myself off as a great artist. The name in my passport was Julian Jorge de la Llata Vizcaíno.

15. I did everything exactly as Chesterton asked.

I handed over a guitar case full of little bags to a man in a green tie and sunglasses with a red bump on his forehead.

16. With the large amount of money I was given, I invested in a blue-and-yellow flowered dress for Mother, a leather jacket for the Toad, and a few parcels of land.

17. When I went to confession, the priest asked me to meet with him later in the afternoon.

18. He explained to me why it was bad to be wallowing in the mire and he promised to help me straighten out my life. I helped him in return with a good-sized contribution.

19. It was very difficult for me to repent for what I had done, but I had to do it, as well as learn to be an acolyte in the church.

20. The Toad was so proud of me that he boasted to all his friends. Almost all of them went out of their way to take communion with me on Sundays.

21. Except for Chacha, whose parents were Evangelists or Muslims and who disliked our traditions.

22. I had a bad spell of luck all of a sudden. I don't know about other people, but for me April is the cruelest month. So many things happened to me, it's hard to imagine. I had a fainting spell during Eucharist, the Toad got malaria, my sheep were stolen, the girl who brought us hyacinths drowned, my crops were flooded, and there was that

horrible silence to be heard on Sundays. The director of my bank died, too.

23. Chesterton explained to me that once you're in the business you can't just quit. I told him what the priest had told me and he told me that was all bullshit and that in his opinion I was no idiot. He spat on the floor and, unintentionally, the spit landed on my shoe.

24. I asked him to let me think about it. First, I consulted my father. He pushed me to accept the deal. Then I spoke with the priest, who told me what life was like in hell. The next day, I decided to reject Chesterton's offer.

25. Mother boasted to everyone how I had refused. In exchange, I received true gestures of love and respect.

26. I was then asked to become the new municipal president. I felt truly flattered. Even Mrs. Dominga gave me her vote of confidence, and she cooked up two stuffed hens to convince me.

27. When the priest found out that I had accepted the position, he gave me his blessing. He asked me to accept my new responsibilities and to have faith in the great judgment to come.

28. I started work in June, already far from fateful April.

29. My new work consisted of handing out food and help to the church community, ordering the hands of the cattle thieves to be cut off, and being

the first in singing the national anthem every Monday. I also had to choose the people to pay for the fireworks for our festivities, and to marry those who should be married.

30. I had seven policemen working for me and people called me every day to say hello and to ask how I had slept. I had my shoes shined in the afternoon and I played dominoes with the ever-serene Ramoncito, the owner of the Hotel Emperador, and his likable friends.

31. A prostitute, one who I had visited several times in my younger years, asked me to help her. She had been accused of robbing hens and geese from the Esternón family. The problem was that Mrs. Argentina Esternón had visited me and also asked me to help her. After thinking it over a little while, I paid for the stolen birds out of my pocket and I gave a gift of a dozen ducks to the prostitute. The priest agreed with my decision and told me that it was the act of a noble soul.

32. One day Chesterton came into my office in a wheelchair. "What happened to you? " I asked. "This," he replied. We spoke about business for fifteen minutes without getting anywhere. He called me a coward and I asked if he knew what hell was like. The fires of hell.

33. During my free time I would knit, especially in the afternoons. I thought about how the best thing for the people in my town was to produce and

to work and to thus maintain our families. To set a good example, I stopped drinking.

34. Mother sold what I knit at a good price and it inspired me to continue. And that's how the months passed.

35. One night I realized that my education was lacking. My wife agreed, and I quit my work as municipal president. I took my family and went to study in the city.

36. We had a going-away party. Everyone got together and hired the San Andrés Mariachis to brighten up the leave-taking.

37. The roast meat dish got the Toad sick. He kept throwing up and he had stomach cramps. When Dr. Merino assured us he was out of danger, we left for the urb, as gentle Ramoncito called the city.

38. If I had remembered, I wouldn't have done what I did, that is, go to the urb in the very month of April.

39. A man with a mustache took all of our money. And then poor Mother fell ill with dysentery and we all wound up in a hospital.

40. The Toad managed to get money for medicine and I got money for food. We made a good team.

41. In the end, in the month of May, we found a good room to live in and a good school for the Toad. Mother got work as a maid and I made ends meet for a while by asking for handouts on the street. Then I started washing cars and later became a salesman.

42. Nonetheless, as hard as I tried to study, I just couldn't. I never understood what you had to do to become a doctor, even though it wasn't all that difficult to get the Toad into junior high school.

43. Then a woman by the last name of Mendizabal explained everything.

44. I didn't become a doctor, but I did become a businessman. I learned how to sell lottery tickets, and then medicines, and then bathroom supplies, and then animals.

45. I traveled to the jungle, hunting monkeys and parrots and baby tigers. I sold them to a guy who in turn sold them to zoos in other parts of the world.

46. Then the Toad got married, left his studies, gave me a grandson named Augustin, and he went to work in the textile industry. Like me when I married his dear mother, he was sixteen.

47. Then a man named Pilz asked me to work with him in my area of expertise, in his country. Mother and I traveled by plane (I have already described elsewhere what it is like to be up in the air).

48. Pilz put me to work trapping animals on his land so he could sell them.

49. Everything was going just fine, since I knew how to trap the animals on his ranch. But the other hunters and I weren't able to communicate, as we spoke different languages, and so we didn't get along. At the nightly parties, they would shove us to one side as if we were animals.

50. Mother told me that this life was becoming unpleasant, even though we ate stew every day. And she missed our little Toad.

51. I was also somewhat depressed and I couldn't seem to lift my spirits.

52. In order to get back to the urb, we had to become thieves. Mother assured me that the priest would not approve of our plans. I promised her that we would go to him for confession afterward and that would take care of everything. And so we began to rob people.

53. No sooner did we get to the urb with our little nest egg then we found out that the Toad had a baby girl. I told him that, under the circumstances, the best thing to do would be to return to our town. He agreed.

54. His friends gave a great going-away party with pork tamales and beer. Cristina, my granddaughter, was sneezing the whole afternoon and finally gave us all her cold.

55. When we returned to our town, that very night they threw us a welcome-back party with sandwiches and tequila.

56. Chesterton, the new municipal president, took charge of the music, and he brought a trio from San Nicolás El Elevado. Mrs. Dominga brought balloons and sweets for the kids. The priest was so pleased with our return, but also so tired, that instead of giving us confession, he left us with three

Our Fathers and ten Hail Marys to absolve us of all our sins.

57. I started knitting, and Mother sold what I knit. The Toad went to work for the pharmacist. The Tack, my daughter-in-law, took care of the kids and cooked for us every day. Her soups made us happy.

58. Things were going very well for us, until the Toad got into a fight and was stabbed to death.

59. Chesterton put the killers in jail and I asked him to let me take care of the matter myself. I believe I must have looked so upset because of the Toad's death that he told me, "Go ahead, do what you have to do." I beat the murderers to death, with the help of a man named the Boiler.

60. Mrs. González told me she had a little job for me. As I was low on funds, I accepted.

61. I had to take her money to the urb and give it to a man with a goatee and snakeskin boots. She assured me it was a very simple deal. I believed her.

62. I did exactly as she had said and there were no problems. After the deal, the man with the goatee said he also had a little job for me if I was interested. "Well, what is it?" I asked. "Just play it cool for a while, then let a blond guy beat you up and take this little bag here."

63. Truth is, the blond guy didn't hit me all that hard. As I had agreed, I let him rob the little bag from me and give me a few smacks. My client gave

me the money we had agreed on and I went to the bus station.

64. When I went to confession, the priest said he didn't understand anything, but that letting myself get hit and robbed of something that wasn't mine was not evil. He told me that next time I should just ask him first. I agreed and he gave me absolution.

65. That night, Mother told me she thought we were going to have another child.

66. With the money I had earned, I threw a party to celebrate. There was so much chicken and mole sauce left over that we had to give it out to the neighbors. Mrs. Dominga, who was going to be our child's godmother, hired the group La Tambora de San Isidro, very well-known musicians.

67. A man with a pair of tiny glasses said he was an anthropologist and wanted to interview me. What he offered to pay me was very little compared to what Chesterton or Pilz or the man with the goatee paid me, but in the end I agreed.

68. He wanted me to tell him about my life, and that's what I did, from the day they killed my parents to the day I wound up in the mire.

69. Cristina asked me again and again to tell her the story of how I killed the guys who murdered her father. She loved to listen to me tell it.

70. Some men came to town to buy up a lot of land. The gentle, very intelligent Ramoncito told all of us in the town to be careful because what hap-

pened to San Nicolás El Elevado might also happen to us.

71. We brought our machetes and our rifles and we ran them right out of town. They were so frightened they didn't even take away the pots in which they had cooked their lunch.

72. Mother blessed me with a little girl. We wanted to name her Antonia, the name of my dear mother, but Mrs. Dominga asked us to name her Carmelita, after her mother.

73. On Holy Thursday, I bumped into the medium-tall man with a feathered hat in a cantina. He was older. He asked me how I was doing. I told him I wasn't doing all that bad, although I was now quite poor. He told me he was a man of money and he could help me. He was called Don Raúl.

74. I helped him bury some family members who had died. He paid me and told me I could count on him when I ran out of money.

75. On April 8 I fell into a ditch when I was chasing a stray goat. Chesterton and Don Raúl paid Dr. Merino to fix my back.

76. On April 10 Mrs. González brought me another strange dessert and asked me for a favor. She wanted me to tell Don Raúl that she would like to meet with him to do business.

77. At first, Don Raúl thanked me for the message, and then after thinking it over he said it would be better if I killed her. I thought about how the

priest would not forgive me if I murdered her, nor would she, but the truth is that my family situation was very bad.

78. With all the money that Don Raúl gave me, I bought several parcels of land and then I sold them to other men who wanted to buy land in our town. The gentle Ramoncito and the priest told me I had a knack for buying and selling.

79. Once the parcels of land were sold, Mother, the Tack, Agustín, Cristina, Carmelita, and I went to San Nicolás El Elevado, as things were heating up a bit in town.

80. After inquiring around, the anthropologist managed to track me down and came to my house to continue with the story of my life. I started inventing things to keep him interested.

81. At that time, the prostitute who had made me a man was living in San Nicolás. I met her in the plaza and she told me she needed money. I gave her all the money I had on me.

82. She also said that if I wanted some extra cash, there was always the Tack. She would take care of everything, and would even bring the money to our house.

83. Well, that's how it was. My daughter-in-law supported us for more than a year with the help of the prostitute, and with the help of Don Raúl, too, who was her best client.

84. Toward the end of March I became nervous.

Another April was coming and I didn't know what surprises it held in store for me.

85. There were many, but all of them good. Don Raúl asked me to bury his dead again, the Tack got engaged to the owner of the largest hardware store in San Nicolás El Elevado, Chesterton offered me a job as a policeman, and Cristina got pregnant.

86. The only bad thing of that dry April was that Mother caught dysentery again and died in bed.

87. I told my daughter-in-law that she had to break off her engagement, as I was now without a woman.

88. At first, the priest was opposed to our marriage, but he wound up marrying us since it was best for everyone. Even the hardware store man understood the situation and he supplied the musicians.

89. As the family members of poor Don Raúl kept dying, I had work giving them their Christian burials and I earned big bucks. So many had died that he no longer looked sad.

90. Then Cristina ended her pregnancy and gave me a great-grandson named Joselito, son of the Boiler, whose first name was also Joselito, and whose last name was Ternero.

91. Later, at the beginning of February, Dr. Merino sent me to Torreblanca for some tests. He told me I had "it." What could I do, I had lived a good life.

92. The priest explained to me that life was like

that. God breathed life into our soul, and there wasn't much one could do when faced with such calamities.

93. I wasn't worried about death so much as about not having enough food to eat the day the Distrustful One, as Mrs. Dominga called death, arrived.

94. The Boiler said if I let him, he would take charge of the family when the Inevitable One, whom he also called the Liberator, arrived.

95. I had become a skeleton and my whole body hurt. My Opponent, as Don Raúl called the door that is death, was already nosing around, waiting for me to give up the ghost that April 2.

96. But then my daughter-in-law informed me she found out she was going to have my child.

97. The Boiler figured that's what made me recover, for I began to knit like mad so my wife could sell what I knit in our town, in Torreblanca, and in San Nicolás El Elevado.

98. My pain went away in July and I put on a few pounds.

99. Chesterton tried to kill me once with his pistol but Dr. Merino saved my life. Then Don Raúl also got pissed off at me and tried to light me on fire.

100. The anthropologist told me he was going to write a book about my life. Truth is, what did I care? I was already what they call a dead man.

abbreviated memoirs of a good-hearted person

I WAS A WEALTHY MAN AT THE TIME.

Minister **** called me on Wednesday and invited me over for a chat. I told him he was naive. He hung up on me. One of his bodyguards came over the next day and pushed me around with excessive violence, but he didn't really hurt me.

Afterward there was a period of calm. I took pleasure in watering the flowers in the garden and playing my flute in the afternoons.

Until Alma showed up at my house. She had been a student of mine in a theater workshop I held months ago (I am a famous playwright). She told me she wanted to talk with me. I said all right. She talked for a just a little while and then she seduced me. She had a split lip.

Alma is one of those women with small feet.

I went with her to the horse races and I didn't win

a cent. Alma, on the other hand, won two small bets. We ate in an Argentinean restaurant where the waiters dressed as cowboys, and she asked me to marry her.

When I told my only (seventeen-year-old) son my plans he said I was mistaken in them, my plans.

Nonetheless, we got married. One day before Alma turned twenty-one.

My father came as an invited guest. He didn't want me to sign the papers nor did he want to meet my new in-laws. He sat there, in his seat, without bothering to find out what the wedding of his only son was all about. I later heard that he had a good time.

The leader of the telephone union, a certain ****, made an appointment to see me. We spoke about the moral fiber of the union leaders and we came to an agreement. Although I thought he was naive, I didn't tell him. But in the end he began to bother me and he left the house a little pissed off.

All because he offered me, in exchange for the child I might have with my wife, a brand-new Mercedes Benz.

At that time, my wife took my father for walks and made sure the gardener took care of the garden. A few days later, the gardener raised a fuss and I had to fire him.

Six months later, my friend, Minister ****, sent me a gift with a card that said that he had just found out about my wedding from another friend, the attorney general. He scolded me for not having told him about the event. Nonetheless, he sent me an authentic fossil wrapped in flowered paper. Alma set it on a small table in the tea parlor.

Small red bumps covered my body. My father told me it was from chronic seafood poisoning, but I hadn't eaten abalone or crab for days. He explained that it was triggered by having eaten too many shrimp and lobsters over the years.

After a week of drinking orange leaf and garlic tea, the bumps went away.

I was there for the birth of the twin girls. It was truly marvelous. It was also something wonderful for Alma, although afterward she became depressed. She threw a wooden horse at me.

As she couldn't produce enough milk for both, I hired a wet nurse to help her with the breastfeeding. Her name was Morita.

At this stage of my life, I didn't understand why the wealth I had been accumulating was decreasing.

Until one day I ceased being, as they say, an affluent man.

Before selling one of my factories, I think it was a soap factory, I appointed myself director. The new owners took me on for a trial period, but as I wasn't fulfilling my duties, I resigned after six or seven days.

The twins grew up and were the best part of my life. I bought them twin toy houses, twin teddy bears, twin beds. Twin dolls just like them.

We went to a spa and had fun in the swimming pool, although one of the twins almost drowned. I met a man in the export business, a Mr. ****, who invited me to do business with him. I consulted with my father and he advised me that it wasn't a good time for exports. "Whatever you do, import," he told me.

I was just about to start importing when I entered the government at the invitation of Mayor ****. I had to work all day in a suit and tie and I came home exhausted. My work consisted of bossing around my employees and dictating letters to be sent to my friends, ministers, and political leaders. One day, a woman made an appointment to ask for work. She seduced me. I gave her the job and let her seduce me, although I didn't continue with, as they call it, the amorous affair. She made a kind of empty hole with her mouth when she kissed.

I ordered the construction of a zoo and I imported elephants, giraffes, wild boars, and llamas, as well as several other species of animals. The twins were fascinated with the beautiful specimens. And people generally enjoyed them, as could be seen by the fact that they threw lots of food at them.

Then I was given a promotion, and I received a great deal of criticism in the daily papers.

One day, Alma acted in a play in a theater under my office's control. I thought it wise to invite the president so he could enjoy it. Utterly naive, he whispered in my ear that having my wife take her clothes off and kiss two men at the same time didn't look right. I responded that I thought his wife was unattractive. He ordered me to come to his office and apologize. I told him there was no reason to, I was sick of being a politician.

That day, one of the twins fell and fractured her finger.

Through my brief experience as a public figure I once again became an affluent man, having signed and deposited a few checks into my own account.

In order to continue being a wealthy man, I decided to invest. My father guided me. He suggested that I buy houses, rent them, then ask for credit from the banks and import gin and apple brandy.

Alma continued taking her clothes off and kissing different guys, one of them black. I believe they chose her to act in such risqué roles on account of her fine body and good diction.

The twins' nanny tried to seduce me with the old ploy that she was a good reader of dramatic works. I listened to her for a while and then I let her take her clothes off. Her breasts were so large I was speechless. She asked me what was wrong and I responded that she had very large breasts. She covered them up indignantly and said she wanted to quit her job as the twins' nanny. I wouldn't let her. We wrestled on the couch a bit and I let her touch me wherever she wanted. In the end, she didn't quit.

At that time there was a huge problem in the countryside, and I was called in to work again in the government. I resolved the problem as well as I could, criticism hailed down on me in the press, and I deposited a few checks into my account and then quit. The president told me he had nothing personal against my wife. I returned the pleasantry, assuring him that I had nothing against his. He offered me the opportunity to be ambassador in **** and I accepted, for the travel and the world experience.

Upon arrival in ****, the twins got the measles and things became difficult between Alma and I. By way of reconciliation, I promised her I'd return to the theater. I staged a production of George Bernard Shaw and it met with moderate success.

Nonetheless, I soon lost my reputation as a dramatist and man of the theater. It turned out that the prince of ****, who had seen my production, invited me to talk with him about Marlowe and I disappointed him. We were eating some tacos when he asked me my opinion. I told him quite naturally that they were a couple of idiots (him and Marlowe).

My criticism of Marlowe in front of the prince turned out to be disappointing and unjust for Alma. The following day she had the leading role in an underground nudist piece taken away from her, and instead she was offered the role of a soldier in a Lope de Vega play.

I scolded myself for my untimely comment.

The people in the embassy were not interested in my problems in the world of theater. They kept demanding that I work in the office signing papers and checks. Minister **** called to ask me to apologize to the prince. I refused.

On my last day in the embassy I played chess with a sickly-looking consul. I beat him with my queen and two pawns.

Although I left foreign relations, I decided we would stay on in **** for a while because the twins liked the parks. But then winter came and they no longer wanted to go out into the street.

Alma loved them and gave them constant attention. I decided then that it was time to return home.

My father had died the year before. One year was such a long time that I couldn't even cry for his loss. My Aunt ****, who had decided to have him cremated and to have his ashes strewn in the Plaza de Armas, told me my father's last words. "Tell my son that he shouldn't be silent when he has something to say, to lie only when it is truly necessary, to invest in flowers, and to teach my grandchildren to respect their ancestors."

I bought thirty-eight acres of land and planted roses of various colors.

I enrolled in a course at the university to get a more in-depth understanding about my ancestors. In the cafeteria, a fellow classmate in anthropology insisted she was in love with me. I hugged her tenderly and told her I was married. Then I bought almost all the books that dealt with my ancestors, quit school, and put together a handsome, useful library.

Alma threw the wooden horse at me again and asked for a divorce. I explained to her that it was my duty to teach the twins, and she gave in.

Twelve acres were a total loss, but the rest yielded attractive profits.

The new government invited me to join their ranks as a cabinet member. I accepted the position of minister of education out of respect for my ancestors and love of my daughters. I built them a school and hired the best teachers. They looked so happy studying history that I enjoyed working just for them.

Then they assassinated the president with a bullet and the guys came and asked me to replace him. I had never thought of the possibility that I would become president of the nation. I accepted for Alma and the twins. I was sure it would please them.

I believe I did much good for the country. I ordered the construction of a giant, blue-colored bridge which is now the pride of the nation. I bought lots of land and many millions of cows so that all families could have free milk. I imported thousands of tons of salami at ridiculous prices. I ordered roses to be planted in several districts. And I started to read the letters that people sent me.

There were so many that Alma and the twins helped me answer them.

At first we personally handled all the people's requests. We were going to bring them the sheep they asked for, to carry out justice, give aid to babies, and give away parcels of land. We soon had to ask for help from the Army and the Red Cross in order to make ends meet.

Our family was an example to the country.

One of my underlings told me to put an end to all the gift giving. I told him the people were happy. He told me there was no more money. I told him I would sell a few things. He told me they were already sold. I asked him why I hadn't been consulted. He responded that it had been necessary. I fired him and hired the twins in his place.

They assured me that the people were pleased with the gesture. They did surveys and wound up selling off everything the government owned.

When I was already beginning to be bored by being president, they killed Alma in an assassination attempt. Two men in suits fired at her with a bazooka as she was leaving the supermarket. My twins were sad. They had been very close to their mother.

As I didn't know to whom I had to resign, the twins and I packed our bags and made up our minds to fly to ****. As we boarded the plane, the pilot told us that the government had been overthrown. Fortunately, we had already packed our bags.

At the airport in **** we met up with my son, who decided to join our flight as he was tired of studying so much. The four of us wished to forget all our misfortunes and setbacks.

When we arrived in **** we were met by Archbishop ****. I hugged him close, and during our walk to the parking lot I confessed that we had fled the country. When he told me that he already knew, I was finally able to relax.

Fortunately, before abandoning my country I had been able to make a few deposits into my checking account. Enough not to have to worry. I bought a farm with some of the money, and we became farmers.

A neighboring farmer by the name of Malibu invited me to her bedroom and then I married her. She was one of those women who have an innie bellybutton and thin eyebrows. She had cows, sheep, and geese. And she had beets, basil, potatoes, and tomatoes growing in her fields.

The twins also got married the same day to my sons-in-law. Since Malibu was well known throughout the region, the wedding was a success. Except for my son who, while eating wedding cake, decided to study mountain climbing.

At first, under the influence of alcohol, his twin sisters lovingly warned him against the useless life of mountain climbers. Then they sided with him and I had to join with them in their enthusiasm and good spirits.

I remember we ate fish at sunrise. I believe it was hake. I also remember how Malibu, at age twenty-five, tried to give womanly advice to the twins (three years her senior) and to their husbands. None of them objected and there were no fights.

We got together on Sundays to roast hot dogs and talk. On one of those afternoons Archbishop **** entertained us by singing pop songs. Later that day, in the bathroom, he asked me to become a member of the academy. With his influence I would be accepted.

The next day, however, I had a heart attack. According to the doctor, I almost died. Malibu sat by my side for four or five nights straight. I loved her.

At that time war broke out and I stocked up. I bought everything so my family wouldn't have to go without. Which never happened as the war ended very soon.

At the insistence of Malibu, I realized I had to do something with the rest of my life. I bought canvases, tubes of oil paint, and brushes. I decided to become an artist. My first painting was a landscape that I sold to a reputable collector at a good price.

Malibu wrote beautiful works for the theater and acted in one of them. People praised her breasts and ass. And for good reason.

One day I lost my sight and I stopped writing. Malibu told me she had bought a new car.

what you need to do is to read kant

OKAY, THAT'S ENOUGH. MY THROAT'S KILLING ME.
The whole fucking night, talking and talking about
meaningless things. With you insisting that I said
something I never said, over and over, until finally I
just had to stop and go and get an ashtray. And even
if I did say it, it doesn't mean anything. Why would
I say something I neither believe nor feel nor mean?
/ Yes, yes, I went for an ashtray, that's true, but what
does that prove? That I'm the monster you say I am?
Enough! It would be better if we just went to sleep
. . . as if nothing ever happened. Ay, but no, no, you
just won't stop. Well then, tell me this, have you ever
read Plato? A dialogue is a dialogue. First, one
person talks, and then the other. One person says
something, and the other person either disagrees or
agrees or else they ask a question. What is not an
option is for each one to just talk and believe that

they are having a dialogue. We aren't conversing with each other, not any more. I could say to you: "The crisis you're going through affects you more than anyone else. How do you expect me to size it up, take it in or straighten it out if you don't even accept that it exists?" To which you might respond, as you already have: "You drink to avoid me." You see? We're talking about different things. You're talking about turtles and I'm talking about the beauty of flowers. Do you see? Plato could teach you things you never dreamed of. He'd teach you how to get along with other people, for a start. If a dialogue exists, there is the possibility of understanding. But this way . . . this way any relationship is impossible. / The fact that I drink has nothing to do with your crisis nor with what you think I'm saying. I drink because I like to. I have always drank and I will continue to do so for as long as I can. Even if you don't like it. / Don't blame your problems on my pleasures. / Addiction? Go ahead, those words don't scare me. "My addiction . . ." You know you should really start with Socrates. The Platonic dialogues are Socratic dialogues. Socrates never insulted the people he talked with, he had no need to. Do you know why? Because he engaged in dialogue. When two intelligent people engage in dialogue they have no need to insult each other. Look at this photograph.

What do you see? / Yes, they're slaughtering a pig,
although I prefer to call it a swine or a sow or a hog.
Pig is what a vulgar person would call it. But, well,
you were born in the countryside and you have the
right to call it a pig. What did you say? / You see,
we were talking about how they're killing an animal
and you had to get stuck on the insult. The photograph is just a conversation piece in order to illus-
trate the advantages of reading Plato. Socratic
dialogue. Communication. None of this, "I said;
you said; I didn't say; how could you think that; of
course I believe . . ." All of that is bullshit. / No, I'm
not joking. I'm absolutely serious. For example, you
could have responded that for you a pig cannot be a
swine, sow, or hog but only a pig, given the fact that
since you were a baby farm girl that is the name by
which you know it. That would have struck me as a
good response. Look at this other photograph.

I'm not fooling around. Give me a little bit of credit and tell me what you see in the photo. / Okay, okay, I'll tell you what it is that I see. I see a man spitting fire. The expression of the people who are watching is interesting. Instead of being amazed by the man's talent, they seem to wish that some accident would stop this disagreeable sight. / I'm not hallucinating. That is *my* interpretation. I said disagreeable because no one could actually like the sight of someone making their living by spitting fire. / Oh, so you like it? You're just saying that to contradict me. Of course you don't like it, you told me so. / When? Don't try to play games with me. How am I going to remember when? I don't know, I don't remember, but I'm sure you told me so. / Of course I know you. I know you better than you think. Better than you know yourself. / More insults? You see, the way you treat me is to insult me. Don't break glasses. Do you think that by breaking glasses you're going to gain something? Fine, if you want to break them, go ahead, I'm not going to stop you. What an easy thing it would be to understand each other. Everyone does it. Like Socrates and Phaedro. I think it was Phaedro. Admit it, instead of fighting with each other, wouldn't it be better to understand each other like the Greeks, like Socrates and Phaedro? / If you don't stop, I'll show you that I can be insulting and break things, too. Keep pushing me and you'll see a side of me that you haven't seen before. / Oh, so I insult you, do I? Come on, my dear, let's be adults. Please. / That's an insult? I didn't say it to provoke you. I just think you're not mature enough to carry on a friendly conversation. Come on, I'm being objective. I'm not trying to impose moral judgments. It's quite easy to be immature. You don't have to be ashamed about it. There are immature people who manage to reach eighty. / No, I'm not drunk. I know exactly what I'm saying to you and I could back it up tomorrow at breakfast. / Of course we're going to have breakfast. No, we're not going to break up over a bad conversation. Don't be so melodramatic. "I want a divorce." You've been watching too much television. Just because you're immature doesn't mean we're going to stop living together. You can still grow up. It's just a question of time. I'll help you. / Saying that I'm the immature one is just deflecting the conversation elsewhere. Prove it. For example, tell me of one instance in which I insulted you. That would be a proof of immaturity. / Stop laughing like an idiot. Your irony is puerile. / Puerile means you're being a child.

/ Why did I marry a child? Don't try to confuse me. When I first met you, you weren't as odd as you are now. Well, not odd but . . . unaware, infantile. I think your mother screwed you up. / Yes, your mother. She spends the whole day giving you advice about how to treat your husband, as if I were just another husband. That is, just a regular, everyday husband. / No, I don't want to get your mother mixed up in this, but there's no avoiding it. One of these days it just had to come out. She's the one who's destroying your life. / No, I haven't the slightest idea what your father was like, but I'm sure she must have had real problems with him. / I've seen it lots of times, you don't have to show me his photograph.

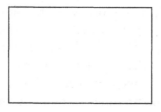

What do you mean, what do I see? Now you're the one being Socratic? Okay, fine, fine. I see a man in his forties, without a care in the world, without a goal in his life. / Fuck it, I have a right to say what I think. Or at least what I see in a photograph. / Yes, I realize you must have a different view of things.

He's your father. But that doesn't give you the right to limit my freedom of opinion. I could lie to you, if that's what you want. Okay, I see a loving man, worried about the well-being of his daughter. / No, I'm not fooling around. It's the same as if I were to tell you that you don't have the right to see a pig where I see a swine or a sow or a hog. You have the perspective of someone who grew up on a farm while I'm a man of the city. Neither is better than the other. Do you understand? Do you see where I'm heading? / What? In case you haven't noticed, you've also been drinking. All this talk about alcoholism, you're just projecting. You're the one who's being damaged by drinking. If you think you can defend everything you said tonight in the morning, just imagine me. I have always been able to defend what I say. Always! I never try to get off by saying, "Forgive me, I must have been tired. . . ." / I am not making fun of you! I know it might have sounded like that, but I wasn't trying to imitate you. Forgive me, if that's what you want me to say, forgive me, really, I had no intention of making fun of your whining voice. / And I didn't mean to make that face. It just happened. I already asked you to forgive me, isn't that enough? / Oh, now it's divorce again. Okay, if that's what you want, I'll give you a divorce. But you'll see, tomorrow we're going to have breakfast together as if nothing ever happened, you'll go shopping with your mother and I'll go to work. / Well, what else do you do? You always go shopping with your mother. I'm only saying what I see. / Don't be an idiot, what I meant to say is that tomorrow will be just like any other day. It was not my intention to criticize you. Not you nor your mother. Her activities, if you can call them activities, are none of my business. What's more, you can both go shopping whenever you want. When it comes down to it, I'm the one who works. . . . And it's not that I'm complaining. . . . Although, if you think about it, just what will you do if we get divorced? I mention it so that you can see that your "I want a divorce" is just drivel. / Oh, so you think you'd get alimony? Where do you think we live? There are laws in this country, and don't you go believing that they exist to protect do-nothings. / I'm not saying you're lazy. What I meant to say is that if you divorce me, you're going to have to get a job. / I know you can, I know you're not a good-for-nothing. I'm just trying to make you understand that an argument like the one we're having right now does not end in divorce. In the whole wide world there has never been a single time that a marriage has broken up over such foolishness. These things happen. Like this. . . . All married people fight. All of them, understand? And usually over the same stupid things. In China, Japan, Uruguay. Which is why I suggest that the best thing to do is stop fighting, go to bed, and in the morning, by breakfast time, we'll have forgotten everything that happened today. Without any hard feelings. . . . Look, look at this photograph of our wedding. What do you see?

Look at it. It's not going to hurt you to look. You've seen it a thousand times. I'm only asking you to look at it now so you'll forget about the divorce and we can go to sleep. It won't cost you anything. Come on, give me your hand. Everything's going to be just fine. Come on now, give me your hand. / There . . . you see? It's so easy. You see, there's no reason for us to fight. . . . These fights happen, it's natural. . . . Give me a kiss. . . . We'll finish this once and for all. / Okay, then let me kiss you. I'm not too proud to make peace with you. / That's it . . . that's it. . . . / No, let me take your shirt off. . . . Slowly, there's no rush. Do you remember our first time? I remember perfectly. You had on your red-striped shirt. . . . Yes, you took it off. . . . Remember how I kissed your breasts . . . like this . . . / Yes, I was hornier than I've ever been. / Of course I was hornier than I've ever been. Monica never meant anything to me. I don't know why you're so obsessed with Monica. It was never more than a one-night stand. . . . Anyway, don't tell me you weren't wild about that gringo. / I know his name is Martin. But you were wild about him, you told me once. / Well, okay, I just wanted to hear you say it. Come on, take your clothes off and let's go to our room. / Here, in the kitchen? Well, if that's what you want it's fine with me, it's just that I thought our bed would be more comfortable, but . . .

There, see, I told you, all we had to do was to look at our wedding photo and we wouldn't be angry anymore. Did you like it? I was remembering our first time together. / No, you weren't the one who took the initiative. Remember, I was the one who hugged you. / What do you mean I wasn't all there? I knew we were going to make love from the beginning. I saw it in your eyes. You were like a dog in heat. What's more, I'm sure you would have liked to do it right away. / Well, I say it because that's the way I felt, or can't I say how I feel? / I'm not being aggressive, I swear. That's just how things happened. Try to remember. / How could you think I'm calling you a whore? If that were the case, do you think I'd have married you? No, my dearest, the truth is, I think what you need to do is to read Kant.

people are strange

MY GRANDSON AND I ARE TWO HOLLOW HUMAN beings. Between fleeting victories and unforeseen calamities, between useless conversations and failed suicide attempts, our lives have been lived in vain.

That's the way we are, and that's the way we've been, my grandson and I.

I feel bad, for my part, that he inherited the sickness (or rather, the rotten gene) from me, and I feel bad, on his behalf, that he let himself be captivated by the advice of a loving grandfather (meaning, that he let himself be influenced by me).

BESIDES both being hollow, my grandson and I both share the same damned disease, a disease that struck me at seventy and him at eighteen. We both know how and more or less when we are going to die. As far as the how, we have been informed that it will not be very pleasant, although some violet-colored pills that taste like paella might help to ease the pain. The when will almost coincide, as he will die at the end of August and I at the beginning of October.

As I will be the one to bury him, we've talked a lot about his funeral and we have already made certain arrangements, such as: the site of his final dwelling place (a very picturesque cemetery); the design and color of the coffin (a carpenter friend has already built it); the wreath; the newspaper obituary; his epitaph ("Here lies a hollow man"); and the moral support I will have to give to the mourners. In addition, we have agreed that I will not cry over his death.

Nonetheless, the problem that has most plagued us over the years is that we might arrive at the End with empty hands, as empty as those of that old man who once asked both of us for money. An old, sad man, despite the fact that he only suffered from leprosy. "A hopeless case," my grandson said to me as he gave him a few bills, "on the same waiting list as the one we're on. Isn't that so, Grandfather?"

My grandson is presently twenty-two years old and I am seventy-four. He has a child and an understanding wife; both are agreeable and good-looking. He is the owner of a tool factory (pliers, hammers, wrenches, and other things, like saws). His house (which he owns) has a three-car garage and four or five bathrooms. My granddaughter-in-law adores him and my great-grandchild loves to play hide-and-seek with him. He adores mole and tostadas, he likes talking about liberal issues, and he admires women who speak without spitting.

That is a brief account of my grandson. A successful-looking man, somewhat intelligent, while at the same time profoundly insubstantial.

Exactly like me, for I am quite the same in that respect. I am a vain old man without much enthusiasm. I have lost almost all my hearing and every night I worry about what I'll have for dinner (which is almost always composed of pears, bananas, apples, and melons). My fortune (which I have, in fact, willed to my wife and my great-grandchild, in equal parts) is not great, although sufficient enough to assure a decent future for both my heirs. But that's all.

There is nothing more I can tell you about my poorly lived life except, of course, the fact that I am a retired police officer. I had a reputation as a good torturer, something that is completely false. The fact that I could almost always get people to cough up information was because I infected them with my boredom and they wound up spilling the beans.

NOT long ago, my grandson and I went to physical therapy together. He helped put my shoe onto my prosthetic device and eased me into my regulation underwear. He urged me on in my routine with kind words and injected me with my daily shot. I wanted to encourage him in like kind, but one of the therapists interrupted our conversation and skillfully solved the problem. She installed my grandson's prosthesis, put a diaper in his underwear, and smoothly inserted the needle into his vein. Then she led both of us out onto the dance floor where we danced for more than an hour.

Miss Du Barry was especially active and flirtatious that day.

An hour and a half later, my grandson and I were sitting and talking in a loud bar named Vistahermosa. The place was decorated with watercolors of waves and seahorses, which made us both very nostalgic.

Every time we came here, we left our prostheses on so as to not bother the other clients, and they almost always assumed that we were basically normal.

My beloved grandson once again expressed his great worry about meeting death with empty hands, and then made a few suggestions. "Grandfather, you will forgive me for what I am going to say, but . . ." he hesitated before continuing, "Why don't you screw Miss Du Barry? I'm sure she likes you. Don't you think so?"

For obvious reasons, my descendant's question opened a wound in the hereditary guilt I carry on my conscience. I knew I couldn't let him down.

Nervously, I said, "Sure, why not?" I proposed that I would pay for the device he would soon have installed on him and I accepted the challenge to give Miss Du Barry a call.

And that's what I did. I called the lady in lust right away, and later I covered the cost of the hook that my beloved grandson would have to use when his already decayed member was amputated.

I DIALED the number of my lover-to-be and, very decently and graciously, she invited us to her chalet. When we arrived, she told us she thought we were wonderful.

We were impressed with the friendly generosity she showered upon us, as well as the sumptuousness of the accommodations. We ate some delicious things that resembled shellfish and drank French wine. Afterward, we went out onto the terrace and spoke about art. Then we went to sleep, each in our own room, until eleven-thirty in the morning. Before falling asleep, several servants aided us in the nightly routine of readjusting what was left of our bodies and in administering our medicine and suppositories. This was done with such experience and grace that the unguent they rubbed on me reminded me of the silken hands of Dr. Maigret.

THE next morning, while we were eating a breakfast of fruit, yogurt, and salmon, my grandson asked me in a whisper if I had screwed the lady during the night. I confessed to him that the opportunity had not presented itself, and that's the way things were to be between us. Like family.

Nevertheless, two minutes later the whole scene changed. As Miss Du Barry was hot to trot, she lowered me into the pool, prostheses and everything, and wrapped me in her lasciviousness. And that was that. We made love a couple of times, until I was exhausted and she was satisfied and (in the words of my grandson) very much in love.

I felt very good about myself for not letting my dear grandson down.

OUR fleeting happiness soon evaporated. We returned to our respective houses with empty hands and without appetite. For my part, I hinted to my wife that I had spent the night in Du Barry's house, knowing that this would give her something to boast about to her friends, but also knowing it would sadden her a little.

For his part, my grandson told his wife we had gone to the horse track and that we had fallen asleep, like so many other times. "Still empty?" my granddaughter-in-law asked him. "I have no idea. Why do you keep pestering me?"

In the middle of these inane marital squabbles, death was overtaking us, and yet we still hadn't found something to give it some dignity. In the end, the satisfaction my grandson received upon my having screwed the lady, as well as my own for having given him this satisfaction, meant almost nothing, just a tiny package to take to the great beyond with our heads held high.

THE leaves of the calendar continued to fly away to the rhythm of Tchaikovsky until the much-feared (or awaited) August, the month of the impending death of my grandson, overtook us. During that time, the doctors amputated one of his hands and installed the chrome hook we had shined so well. We spent two nights with Miss Du Barry (each of us taking turns in the swimming pool), invented sophisms, and each lived alone with our own uselessness. Our own bitterness.

One afternoon, during therapy, he asked me: "Grandfather, is there anything after death?" "No," I answered with more assurance than knowledge. As if he hadn't heard me, he continued. "Do you think our spirit gets a second chance on Earth, or might there be a second life for those of us who couldn't finish this one successfully?" I responded once again with a more definitive negative, although the truth is, I wasn't at all sure.

On August 16, my grandson had a stroke and certain parts of his organism atrophied, though I don't remember exactly which ones.

Later, when he recovered, we met in the park to

discuss what had happened. "If it isn't today, it'll be tomorrow, or the day after," I predicted. "How do you feel?" I continued. "Is death already . . . well, I don't want to say flirting with you . . . but is it . . . you know?" "Yes, Grandfather," he answered, with a beer in his hand, "I can feel it coming. And I can assure you that it doesn't look as aggressive as your wife, if you'll pardon me for saying so."

I was truly relieved.

ON August 21 my grandson suffered a sudden enthusiasm. He started to dance with his son like a madman, sang two ballads, and then went into the kitchen to cook the squid he had bought the night before. I was in charge of opening the bottle of wine and telling jokes. We ate, all talking at once, until exhaustion overtook us.

ON August 29, before the amputation of one of my arms, my grandson predicted that there would be no deaths in the family to grieve over (referring to the two of us). Our wives were infected by his unexpected optimism and they began to sing madrigals and bake cookies.

And my unfortunate heir was right insofar as September 15 came and went and we were both still alive.

Miss Du Barry, who had heard about my grandson's prediction, organized a masked ball in our honor.

On October 1 we went to the hospital together. We complained to Dr. Maigret about his prognosis (regarding my grandson), and he seemed surprised. "Don't worry," he said, "it's imminent. Maybe tonight, or tomorrow afternoon. Trust me, you're about to take a trip without luggage, if you know what I mean."

Then he deigned to acknowledge my presence. "And you," he said, pointing at me, "I wouldn't fool myself about making it to Christmas. I tell you because I respect you. I mean it. But as to the fact that death is hovering around you, no one would dare contradict me. I can almost smell it, and my sense of smell isn't even all that good."

WE all got together that night at Miss Du Barry's house to talk about death and its consequences. My elderly wife commented that human beings are like termites or sunflowers, we just die and that's that. My granddaughter-in-law took exception to what was said, which she felt was thoughtless and without foundation. She responded: "When we die, our spirits will float around for a while until they encounter a kindred organism, whether it be an anteater, a jacaranda tree, a Texan, or a petty thief."

Miss Du Barry, after popping three bottles of champagne and inviting us to imbibe, brought out her own idea of how things were. "For me, true life begins at death. I don't know why, but I can picture all of us playing blackjack in a casino, a . . . what's the word? . . ." She searched earnestly for the adjective, until she finally hit on it. "Celestial. Yes, that's it precisely, a celestial casino."

Death. The proximity of death made us say such stupid things that day that the pope himself would have been rolling on the floor in a fit of laughter.

By way of ending the gathering, my grandson added: "I hope that some of you are right." "I don't know if what we have said," his wife added, "applies to someone so . . . so hollow. Do you know what I mean?" "I know all too well," my grandson responded. "That's what I'm afraid of."

ON October 22 or 23, both still alive, we enrolled in medical school with the idea of beginning a career. We were accepted as regular students and on the first day of classes we arrived with our books under our prosthetic devices.

It was a truly wonderful week.

We learned a lot about the human body, listened to the hearts of our classmates, ate in the university restaurant, and went to several demonstrations.

My grandson was lucky. One of our classmates was filled with desire. One night, they asked if I would help join their bodies together, without all the complicated cables, chains, bulbs, and transistors of which my descendant's body was composed.

She was a very fleshy woman.

The bad part came the first Sunday in December, when the vomiting and the itching in the spine began.

On house call, Dr. Maigret took our blood pressure and applied a thermometer and stethoscope. He then put on his best ancient Greek physician face and assured my grandson and I that we would be crossing the river at any moment. My beloved wife hugged me and my grandson's wife gently encircled his neck in her arms.

Tired of singing again and again "It's Nothing More than a Good-bye," we finally fell asleep around four in the morning.

UPON awakening, after unsuccessful attempts to revive her, Dr. Maigret sadly announced that my granddaughter-in-law had passed away.

I can tell you that we were left speechless and without appetite.

Our faithful physician put on his best King Lear face and said: "She died a natural death, as they call it. The heart has its little shocks, doesn't it." Then, transforming himself into Lady Macbeth, after having drunk a shot (the size of a juice glass) of mezcal, he said: "I am terribly sorry."

WHEN I saw the look of grief on my grandson's face after receiving such unexpected news, I felt so terrible that I thought my time had also arrived. I cursed the Fearful One and asked (convinced) that he take me to his kingdom. My grandson also felt that death was clamoring for his presence.

But it was not to be. We buried the deceased, celebrated Christmas and the New Year, and wrapped ourselves in the security of knowing that there was at least one more January awaiting us, despite the fact that by that time our true bodies were composed merely of trunk and head.

Françoise, the desirous and heavy-set classmate from the medical school, increased her carnal desire for my grandson.

She invited us to the atelier of her mansion, slipped out of her costly clothes, and then paraded her large naked body before our unblinking eyes.

I helped them accommodate themselves so they could comfortably satisfy their sexual appetite. In order to do that, I had to help them avoid several obstacles that interfered at such key moments as petting, penetration, orgasm, and hygiene.

After the workout, exhausted and fulfilled, they congratulated my natural ability for arranging things.

I am proud to have known how to direct such an out-of-tune orchestra.

AND what can I say about the tireless Miss Du Barry? She dedicated herself to making love to us in the swimming pool, first to my grandson, then to me, two or three times a day.

In her case, the intervention of a third party to bring the amorous act to a happy completion was unnecessary, especially as under the circumstances (in the pool), it would have been a bit uncomfortable and overly chlorinated.

BECAUSE of all this, our feared and announced death little by little became diluted in the vegetable soup of passion we ate daily.

In moments of rest, we drank champagne with my decrepit wife and my robust great-granddaughter. Sometimes we played friendly games of blackjack and sometimes we discussed our artificial organs, more as a familiar topic of conversation than as a Greek tragedy.

Although still without that famous package between our hands that would transform our hollow lives into something transcendent, we were relatively lucky and horny.

UNTIL tragedy once again distracted us from our feelings. My great-granddaughter drowned in the bathtub and we were once again in mourning. Our hearts were heavy with bitterness and depression.

I suppose that Maigret wanted to help us endure, but we all knew that it was a useless venture. Deaf and blind, dismembered and sad, my grandson and I decided to fight our fate no longer.

We stopped taking the paella-flavored pills and

refused shots and suppositories. We made a point of eating watercress salad and curried chicken (dishes prohibited by Maigret). We decided not to cover our decaying body parts (an ear and an eye of my grandson, my nose and my tongue) with useless prosthetic devices.

IN April, we asked one of the servants of the exquisite Du Barry to unhook the prosthetic devices that we still had on, and then we rolled around on the deck until we fell into the pool.

We imagined how my hysterical wife (who was watching the scene with her tenth Bloody Mary in hand) would surely complain about something as we felt the water violently entering our lungs.

We also managed to feel how Miss Du Barry tried in vain to seize us and drag us back toward the surface, toward life.

FORTUNATELY, my grandson's wife was right. Today I am a Texan who owns a bar, my grandson is a poor pickpocket, his wife is growing in a public park, and my great-granddaughter is a robust anteater who I visit in the zoo on Sundays with my three small children.

One of them, Benjamin, has inherited my disease.

Next week, I am going to install a modern apparatus in his reproductive member.